DISCOMBOBULATED

KATHERINE BACCARO

iUniverse, Inc.
Bloomington

Discombobulated
Collected Short Stories

Copyright © 2010 Katherine Baccaro

This is a work of fiction. All of the characters, names, incidents, organizations, and dialogue in this novel are either the products of the author's imagination or are used fictitiously.

iUniverse books may be ordered through booksellers or by contacting:

iUniverse
1663 Liberty Drive
Bloomington, IN 47403
www.iuniverse.com
1-800-Authors (1-800-288-4677)

ISBN: 978-1-4502-7401-2 (pbk)
ISBN: 978-1-4502-7402-9 (cloth)
ISBN: 978-1-4502-7403-6 (ebk)

Printed in the United States of America

iUniverse rev. date: 11/20/2010

For my real sister, MARY LOU

BORBORYGMUS

AT THE FAR END of the bar at Foleys a clique of young men was competing for the burp championship of the night. Dermot's lip curled in disgust. He was a young man himself, but he could not remember ever having been that young or so lacking in proper deportment. Youth was no excuse. He considered such demonstrations to be a public affront. Yet the young men continued with their boorish contest. They had the nerve to gaze about contentedly at the other occupants of the bar, as if hoping for applause or audience participation.

Dermot himself was so averse to the kind of vulgarity and gutter language that prevailed in his daily environment that he had mounted in his office a campaign to ban the use of obscene words and indelicate expressions, and Dermot McGreevy carried some weight in the work place, too. He was the youngest executive trainee in the history of the company. With good cause his immediate boss called him Brain Boy. Everyone expected that he would soon ascend to the highest executive position. His opinion was respected. People were actually avoiding the use of four letter words now. He hadn't heard one in quite a long time.

At thirty-seven Dermot had reason to be pleased with himself and with the life choices he'd made. Polite and proper, he was a respectable member of society, the joy of his old mother's heart. His salary was adequate and likely to increase. He derived extra satisfaction from his after-hours hobby of taxidermy. This avocation also provided him with a nice little side income. He was the only taxidermist in town. Though not as beautiful as a movie star he was handsome enough to attract women and virile enough to please them. There was quite a large steno pool at his office. Dermot noticed that a satisfying stir, a kind of fluttering surrounded him whenever he passed the girls.

But no one at Foley's knew this.

Except Agnes Pflieger who was sitting next to Dermot at the end of the bar. Agnes was one of the stenographers at Dermot's office. Dermot had invited her for a drink mostly because she was one of the last girls. He had dated almost everyone else. Agnes was not a particularly pretty girl. Dermot had already used up all the prettier ones. She had a big nose and a slight turn to her left eye but he thought he'd give her a try. She had a certain something that might prove interesting. They had been having a quiet conversation before the boys began with their contest.

"Agnes, do you have a middle name?" Dermot asked her. He totally hated the name Agnes and was searching for some more palatable tag to call her by.

"Yes, I do," she replied. "It's Mabel."

This did not please Dermot. If there was a female name he hated more than Agnes it was Mabel. He would simply have to dream up an elegant nickname for her.

"My friends call me Aggie," she added.

Worse and worse, he thought.

It was at this point in the conversation that the serious belching began. Dermot could barely speak, drowned out by the ugly vibrations filling the air. Apparently the champion was not to appear this evening. They continued with some mediocre burps for some time and then they were silent, undoubtedly storing up gas for the next round. Then the silence was shattered by a bombastic interruption.

BANG! BRRRACK! BURRRACK! BANGKKGK! BRRACK!

Unexpectedly this fusillade, a positive salvo of what almost seemed like gunshot, rent the air.

Everyone looked at Dermot. He was standing by the bar. He was caught there with a horrified expression on a face that was rapidly turning bright red. There was no doubt where the noise had originated. It came from Dermot McGreevy! To make matters worse the boys at the other end of the bar, obviously misinterpreting the sound as another of their favorite bodily noises, applauded.

It was terrible. Dermot was turning redder than a radish. He thought he might faint. He glanced at Agnes Pflieger. She was doubled up, hitched over with obscene laughter. Dermot thought he might die. Feeling around for excuses, he managed to terminate the date. Under the circumstances it was easy enough to claim an illness was beginning deep inside him. He put Agnes in a taxi, simply telling her he did not feel well. She gave him a quizzical look.

But, except for embarrassment, he did feel well. Well enough. He could think of no physical reason for the eruption. As he drove home he pondered the horror of the thing. More and more he had lately become aware of the exaggerated rumblings in his gut. Tonight sound had come out loud as a pistol shot. He was ashamed and distressed by the incident. And that was not to be the end of his suffering.

The very next day in the office a meeting had been called to discuss payroll changes for the company, a very serious matter. Jules Taggert, the leader of Dermot's section, had prepared a preliminary plan that he had earlier distributed to the young executives. "What do you think of my notes, guys?" he said. "Brain Boy, I'd especially like your opinion." And just at that moment Dermot's inconstant stomach let loose a loud and flushing sound. It declaimed, "SSSCHT! SSCHSITT! SHHHCHITT!"

Mr. Taggert's face darkened. "Well, I certainly appreciate your frank and forthright opinion," the boss said insincerely, "but I must say I am rather surprised at your language." The sarcastic note was audible.

There was a long pause. Dermot grew dizzy. He felt the world whirling around his head. He looked sidewise.

Sitting in the stenographer's place was Agnes Pflieger. She was wearing an insolent smile. Dermot felt damned by it.

"Especially," Mr. Taggert continued, "since you have been the arbiter of clean language in the office for the past few months. I, personally, am relieved that all those limits are off. Now we can all talk any fucking way we feel like talking." Everyone was laughing now. Especially Agnes Pflieger.

Dermot walked out chastened and humiliated. He was uncomfortable. He began to wonder if his clothes fit right. His jacket seemed a bit large. Was it baggy? He had put on a bright red tie in the morning. Perhaps that was a mistake. Everything felt wrong. Maybe his shirt was coming out of his pants. That red tie probably just looked silly now. The memory of that audacious girl laughing at him especially riled him.

It was Friday. That night he chose to stay home pondering his problem. What could be causing this repeated embarrassment? He had not eaten anything untoward. His health was optimum. Now he listened hard. His stomach was quiet. Of course it was – no one was around to hear it.

Dermot began to feel somewhat encouraged. Perhaps the siege was over. He decided to call his mother. The world might laugh at him but she would understand. She would understand how miserable he was feeling. Perhaps she could suggest a remedy, but she was not at home. He left a greeting. He did not know what kind of explanatory words could express his actual dilemma.

Saturday morning Dermot had an appointment. Celia Cavendish was coming over. He had a pretty good idea of what the visit was about. Celia had an ancient and incredibly ugly little dog, Robespierre. Its breed was unknown. It bit. As far as Wilmot was concerned she should have named him Rasputin. He didn't like the little beast. Of late it had been sick. Dermot was sure the appointment had something to do with the animal.

Sure enough Celia Cavendish floated in on a river of tears. Robespierre had kicked the bucket. She placed the disgusting little corpse on the table. She cried so hard she was incomprehensible. As a specimen of the fair sex Celia was not very appealing. Now the waterworks had turned her pie face purple and mottled. Dermot, somewhat experienced in pet fatalities, let Celia cry. He took her hand in false sympathy. She'd want to have the mutt embalmed. He wondered if he was up to preserving the ugliness of the beast. He might stuff the cadaver but nothing could ever memorialize its pervasive stink. He patted her hand. Celia shuddered down to silent mourning when suddenly a sound issued from Dermot's ventral region. "HA HA," it said, very clearly. And then, "AH HA HA! HA HA HA HA!" Raucous laughter rang out as if someone in there was having the highest of high old times.

"Scoundrel!" Celia shouted. "What do you think you are, you deplorable, cruel, low-down excuse for a human being!" Sputtering and muttering the most devastating imprecations, Celia Cavendish picked up Robespierre and banged out the door.

Despondent, Dermot sat in the front room of his apartment staring out the window. He watched Celia stomping furiously to her car. Every few steps she looked back at his window. He could see her lips were moving in continual rebuke. He knew now that not only was he at the mercy of his stomach but that his stomach was inimical to him. The day was bright and beautiful but gloom pervaded Dermot's world.

The squeal of the phone made him jump. It was his mother responding to his previous night's call.

"Dermy," she began.

A shudder ran down his spine. He hated that nickname. "Mother, what's wrong?"

"Nothing. Why?"

"Well, you only call me Dermy when you are angry with me. Are you upset?"

"Not at all." She laughed. "I am blissfully happy. Are you upset, Sonny?"

Oh, he so wanted to tell her. Dermot was on very good terms with his mother and on this day he would not have minded the comfort of her maternal voice. But it was so hard to begin. He lacked the vocabulary to describe his problem. "Mother, you see, I am being tortured by sounds from inside me..."

"What, Dermot? You say you are hearing things?"

"Not hearing things, there are actual sounds. They are out to get me."

"You are hearing voices?"

"No. Sounds. Disembodied sounds. No, embodied — from the body. Of me."

"Disembodied sounds!" She did sound concerned, as if she were about to pack him off to a psychiatrist.

"No. Nothing. Never mind. I was just being facetious," he declared, trying to calm her down, and it worked. He stammered through the rest of the conversation. His mother invited him to Sunday dinner and rattled on to him about problems and situations that were of no concern to him. He listened very hard. He was not listening to his mother but to the troubles within. All was still. Silence reigned. The core of his body was quiet.

A face kept intruding on his thoughts. It was not the dappled face of Celia Cavendish, nor was it the angry face of Jules Taggert, but it was the mocking face of that sniggering girl, Agnes Pflieger. Perhaps she was a demon that needed to be exorcised.

Impulsively, he phoned her.

"Hello, Agnes. This is Dermot McGreevy. I was just wondering if you would like to go out to dinner tonight."

Most girls would have jumped at the chance. Agnes didn't answer right away. After a longish pause she said, "Oh, I'm sorry. I just can't."

"Do you have another date?"

"Well, no. Not that. I just don't want to go out with you, Mr. McGreevy."

Incredible! Agnes Pflieger was refusing him! She was putting him at a distance by calling him "Mr. McGreevy." It was unbelievable. Of course, there had to be an explanation. Could it be the gunshot episode at Foley's on Thursday evening? "Agnes, really, I'm so sorry about what happened the other night. I want very much to make it up to you. I promise, nothing like that will happen ever again." But it might. How could he know?

"No. It's not that, Mr. McGreevy. That kind of thing wouldn't bother me at all. I just don't think we have anything in common. It's not your fault, but I just don't really like you."

Dermot was shocked. How insolent she was. How unkind! Yet he was determined to have his way. He wanted to take her out. In his mind he now associated his crisis with this girl. She was in at the outset. He thought he would wine her and dine her as he had done with so many other girls. Then he would drop her, let her try being embarrassed and humiliated as he had been. In the insanity of the moment Dermot even imagined that after she fell in love with him (he'd make that happen) he would disassociate himself from her publicly and loudly and drop her in as open a place as possible, maybe even at the office. There was that, of course, the office. He was her superior there. She probably liked having a job. Suggesting subtly that her employment might be affected, Dermot continued to importune her. Finally she surrendered.

On the drive over to Agnes Pflieger's house that evening Dermot plotted her seduction. It was something he knew how to do. He had done it before. He well understood the frailty of the female heart. When he approached Agnes' front door he felt his confidence returning. He stood with feet firmly planted on the threshold of her apartment but just as Agnes opened the door his renegade stomach announced, "FWARK! FRWCK FWWWUCKM MMM! FWAAWK ME!"

"How dare you!" Agnes cried. She slapped his face. "It'll be springtime in hell before that happens. You're a pig and a hypocrite, Dermot McGreevy!" she announced as she slammed the door.

Alone and disconsolate he filled his desolate hours with brooding until the night passed and it was time to go to his mother's house for Sunday dinner.

Dorothy McGreevy was a pretty, sixty-year-old widow, active in the community. Dermot was proud of her. They were close. Now she took one look at him and gasped. "Dermot! Sonny, what's wrong with you? You look terrible."

It was true. He had looked long and hard at the mirror before coming. His color was ashy. His eyes were vacant. "I had terrible insomnia last night. I didn't sleep at all."

"What would be the reason for that?"

But he couldn't yet bring himself to tell her.

"Oggie's here," she announced cheerfully. "This will give the two of you a chance to get acquainted."

"Oh, great," Dermot said dully. He was not pleased. In spite of his impressive name Ogden George Phillip Anthony Chesterton was a rather common fellow. He was a veteran, had served as a medic during his military years. He liked to give the impression that he had practically been a doctor though Dermot suspected that he had probably done something menial in the service, driving the ambulance or emptying bedpans. Oggie also fancied himself a delightful raconteur. He loved to talk. And the meeting was strained. Oggie knew that Dermot didn't care for him but he was a jovial fellow, not used to this coldness. Both sat in facing chairs in Dorothy McGreevy's front parlor.

That was when it happened again. The machine gun rattling. Bullets!

Twitterings and a viscous sea of giggles. Some mournful crying. A racket arose out of Dermot's middle. Dorothy and Ogden both sat up straight and stared at him.

"Boy, you've got one dandy borborygmus there!"

Dermot almost jumped out of his seat. "What? What did you call it?"

"Borborygmus," Oggie replied. "Yeah," said Oggie. "I ran into a few cases like that when I was in the Army."

"You did?"

"Oh, yeah. Oh, sure, borborygmus. One guy had such a bad case he got booted out of the confessional in his church. The priest thought he was saying, 'God damn it' over and over during the penance."

"That bad?"

"Well, it could be. It could. Take it from me. It could," Oggie said with a knowing air. "Oh, yeah. Another guy's wife wanted to divorce him because his gut kept saying, 'I love you Josephine,' all night long. The wife's name was Maggie."

"I'm cursed! Can nothing be done?"

"Not much. Not much." Oggie smiled. He looked pleased, probably delighted to be consulted. "Borborygmus. It's a normal condition. Probably everyone gets it sometimes. It usually goes away. Not many cases are as extreme as my buddy's back in Fort Huachuca. He was the guy who managed to tame it."

"Tame it? How the hell did he do that? For the love of heaven tell me HOW!" cried Dermot McGreevy, desperation ringing in his voice.

"Well, this guy had had it. He was thrown in the brig for insubordination twice and then he got mad. You're not going to believe this." Ogden chuckled. "He talked to it."

"What?"

"Yeah. Talked to it. That's all. Just talked back to it. Made friends with it. Try it, why don't you?"

Dermot's stomach had just begun babbling idiotically. It seemed to be saying, "Dontchayoudare, Youdondare. "Dermot looked sternly into his lap. "Shut up!" he shouted.

"Hey! Go easy, fella. It's friendship you're after, not submission."

"Shut up," Dermot repeated, but this time more gently, coaxingly. "Please."

The room was silent. The borborygmus had ended. Dermot heaved a sigh. He was again the master of his middle, preparing words to assuage his recalcitrant abdomen. He assumed humility in reasoning with his inner self. Perhaps in time he might even come to enjoy it. Eventually they might even become friends, Dermot thought, though it was somewhat obvious that, unlike Dermot himself, the borborgmus had an excellent sense of humor.

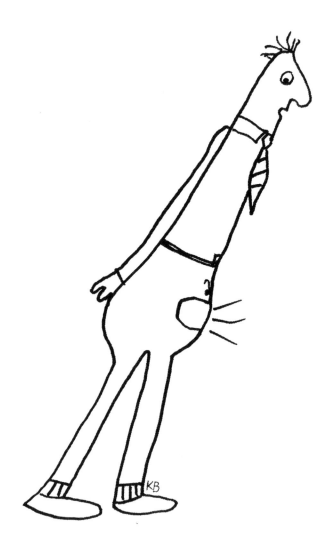

THE MIDDLE DISTANCE

REMEMBER MAE JOHNSON? SHE used to come to the Friday movies with us. We saw some stinkers. We saw that film where a man's brain was put into the body of a great ape and the man got so enraged by the transition that he ranged around the city killing and savaging people right and left. You probably wouldn't remember that. It was so long ago and it was a pretty crappy movie. Anyhow Mae started sobbing inconsolably when a posse of city defenders finally caught up with and killed the monster. For the whole movie they had been chasing him around, missing him over and over again. He'd been hanging around the zoo most of the time but they didn't seem to realize that. They missed the little plot wrinkle that had him in love with some orangutan or other.

Mae cried so loud and hard she started hiccupping and the usher came down and escorted her to the ladies' room so she could calm down. She explained that she couldn't stand it when any animal was hurt, not even a monster. She said that if only kindness had been shown to the beast it would have responded in time, showing the basic humanity that lay within its transplanted brain.

"Yeah, sure, Mae. Try to reason with a murderous ape." I remarked.

"I would," she declared.

And she probably would have if a situation like that ever came up in Bay Ridge, Brooklyn.

"There still were both the basic nature of a violated animal's soul and the finer qualities of humanity within him," she told me, "and they were in conflict — but he could still have been saved."

"Are you kidding? He was killing everything in sight."

11

"He was in love," she said with a really sappy look on her pretty face.

Mae was strange, but mostly likeable. She was quite young then, real cute little girl with a turned up nose and freckles. Just out of high school I think. We kept her in the Friday movie group even though she did tend to cry a lot at movies. She was little, a nice little person. There were some in the movie group that had biting tongues but Mae was infallibly kind. She would always have a positive word. She'd strike up a conversation with anyone. Then she would listen to anyone with a story. With apparent interest she listened to sob stories and medical histories that bored the brains out of most of us. She did seem sympathetic. Truth is, Mae herself was an interesting character.

One Friday we were coming out of the Dyker Theater when a car skidded up on the curb and smashed itself against a window. The occupants of the car were a little roughed up and the police came to gather reports. This happened half the way down 86th Street from where we were standing, right in front of Meyer's ice cream parlor. That was where all the teenage mothers would convene and the sidewalk outside was jammed with baby carriages, some with the babies left in them by their stupid mothers. Mae gave a scream as she could see what was about to happen with the babies there and all. Cops came. The driver of the car missed the baby carriages, just smashed the window of Meyer's. Must have been drunk or on something. Mae could recount every little detail of the incident, even about the car weaving before it crashed. She described a scarf around the woman's neck. She told the cops she recognized that the driver was a woman she had seen before, a woman who used to be an auctioneer at local church bazaars. The cops got plenty of information from Mae. She had observed every detail.

"It was too far from us," I told her. "I really could not see that much."

'In the middle," she said. "It happened right in the middle distance of my field of vision. You were all looking too far down the street. That car came swerving right in the middle distance where I could see it really clearly. My near vision fails me these days and my far vision never was very good but my middle vision still works perfectly." These and other loopy statements that Mae gave out earned her a fair amount of admiration in the Friday group. She was held to be a true original.

That summer I was pretty friendly with her. Most of the people in the movie group were out of town. All I had for socializing that summer was the Friday movies and the tennis courts. Mae was decidedly petite yet she was on a million diets. I wondered about it because she had a really neat small shape that most girls would kill for. About a size three, is my guess. "But they're not exactly that kind of diets," she explained. "I would call them *food regimens*." She was seeing some alternative healers and doctors of the esoteric who advised her and put her on to a lot of crackpot nonsense. One week she ate nothing but avocados and nuts. Another week she declared that she could not eat any food that started with the letter L. She believed in signs and portents. She had some very strong opinions about numbers. She said there were numbers that brought luck and numbers that could damn you to hell, bring curses down upon you. "Once you are numerically scourged you can probably never get out from under."

"You mean like thirteen?" I asked her.

"No. Not at all. Poor Thirteen," she said, just as if Thirteen were a person to be sympathized with. "He always gets a bad rap. Numbers are much more complicated than that." But her eventual explanation was so involved that I decided just to stay away from too many numbers. "Numbers are all around us all the time," she continued, "waiting to exert their direction in every thing that happens in the environment or in the personal behavior of all the occupants of the area. Look around."

I did and, sure enough, there were numbers everywhere. This was in the lobby of the Dyker Theater. Movie dates and times were posted. Prices were up. Quantities were everywhere. There was a huge ad that advertised that their hot dogs here were 13 (thirteen) 13 inches long. I vowed never to choke another one of those down again even though Thirteen, as it turned out, was quite amicable.

The strangest thing of all, however, was her middle-distance theory of space and time. You know, the idea she had that it was only in the middle distance where she could see clearly. "The far distance confounds me and the near distance overwhelms me," she declared. "I want to <u>live</u> in the middle distance."

"Well, you probably do," I said, but truth to tell I had no idea what she was talking about.

Mae told me that she believed there was a veil that existed between the layers of reality. It obscured the truth. Her reality existed in the middle distance but when she tried to approach it the near distance would loom up before her eyes and complicate everything, fuzz everything up. Somewhere, someday, there would be a rip in the near screen and through it reality would come to her anima, allowing her to pass into the middle distance.

I thought her explanation was logical, but crazy. "What if you went too fast and ended up in the far distance?"

I was being facetious but Mae took me very seriously. "No. That would be marvelous. All manner of extraordinary things are in the far distance. Once a hole can break through the separations it can let in all the wonders."

"Like the hole in Alice in Wonderland," I remarked. We were in the car. I was driving her home from the Dyker but I had to stop at the tennis club to pick up something I had left there that morning. When I returned to the car Mae was gazing fixedly over the courts.

"Who is that over there?" she said.

"Big show-offs," I replied. Matt Dugan and Jerry Weissman were battling it out on Court One. They were big bruisers and brutal tennis players. They made tennis seem like a game of war.

"No," Mae corrected. "The guy over there by himself."

I realized she was looking beyond the first section to Court Five where Lanier, all by himself, was practicing his serve.

Lanier was this nerdy kid who had turned up on the tennis courts that spring. He was a colossal pain in the neck, always pestering the good players to play him. He'd had about two tennis lessons and thought he was champion of the world. He didn't actually know the rules of the game. He was even more ignorant of the subtleties and manners involved. He just thought he could bludgeon along. He'd whack balls into the sky, completely out of the court, and think he had done something wonderful. None of the men would play with him and at first he was absolutely snotty about playing with the women, any one of whom could have beaten his pants off. In the manner of young men he was almost rude about it. He was so full of himself. Eventually he realized he would never get a game unless he got friendlier with the girls. In time we even got to like him though he was loopy, full of delusions of grandeur and impractical ideas. He got in several altercations with the park attendant about which way the clay was raked. He claimed the vertical raking enhanced his play and the horizontal rake marks slowed the trajectory of his shots.

Now, out on the court Lanier looked really pretty. He was actually a rather pretty looking boy. He had an amazing head of blonde hair that looked golden in the sun. He also had the most beautiful tennis clothes of anyone that came there, very expensive whites that he'd invested in before he even knew whether he'd play tennis or not. He shone against the background of the red clay court.

"That's Lanier," I said. I could give no particulars, as the most I could say about him was that he was a nerd with nice clothes. "You want to meet him? I'll call him over."

"No," Mae said forlornly. "That could never work."

Without waiting for her answer I had waved to him and there, probably thinking he'd been invited to a game, Lanier Murphy came striding out of her middle distance and full size into her Now.

THE DEPARTMENT OF NOSOLOGY

WHEN TISHA HERMAN AND I were thirteen years old we became dedicated nosologists. We first realized that we shared this interesting preoccupation on the afternoon that we crashed the wedding of Bunny Lobell's sister, Norma.

Down the floral nave came Norma Lobell, dopy as you please. By tradition and all that's holy she should have been following a nose as directed and as proud as the prow of a ship. But her nose was too small. Norma had a tiny little bump where her nose should have been. That pathetic thing could not hold up her large horn-rimmed glasses. Now, wouldn't you think that with that army of sisters and aunts and sundry Lobell in-laws someone would have had the wit to tell her to leave the frigging glasses in the sacristy? But no. She had to wear those giant eyelamps.

Both parents were escorting her. They had her arms in a death grip. Maybe they thought she might skip out. Had she been blind as a troglodyte she would have been steered down that aisle no matter what. As soon as the Lobells released the girl, bouquets, bibles, prayer beads and various holy artifacts were plopped on her, so poor Norma could hardly adjust her spectacles. And they kept trying to slide south The best she could do was set in motion a funny little twitch of her cheeks. She probably thought that was imperceptible.

"Bunny nose," I whispered to Tish. "Not a nose at all. An excuse for a nose."

Tisha gave a subdued little giggle and we turned our attention to the bridegroom. "Spigot," Tish suddenly declared, and she was so right. Roy had a nose that was not remotely like a human nose. It resembled a piece of plumbing, a broken faucet or an end snapped off a drainpipe. "Betcha it leaks," Tisha remarked and the two of us launched into a major giggle fit that got us thrown out of the church.

That was the beginning.

We started sitting in the balcony of the Loew's theater and, in the half light, would peer down the row of profiles beside us. A row of noses – no two alike. That delighted us. "It's better than fingerprints. Cops could identify crooks this way," Tisha declared.

"Yeah. Officer, take his noseprint!" I added.

"We could start a Department of Nosology."

It was around then that we started cataloging noses. We had a big speckled notebook. On the first page I wrote BUMPTIOUS. We started a list of bumptious nosers. No sooner had we begun than we realized the system could not work that way. Every bumptious nose was different from every other. Their common bumptiousness was not description enough. There was nothing to do but list each person individually with the proper nasal adjectives. The list would go something like this:

Johnny Petrans – potato, boiled and peeled

Marykay Howard – zigzag, veering toward the left breast

Drusilla Enth – High Bridge of Sighs. We liked that though it wasn't very descriptive. Later Tisha changed it to *High Bridge of Sneeze* or, sometimes, *High Bridge of Schnozz.*

Oh, we were having fun with it. We even included the teachers. Ms Wilkins was *Bigbugbulb,* and Mr. Turner – *Reddishradishrose.*

Some of the gang got wind of what we were doing. That's when we learned some main truths about noses. First: just about everyone thinks noses are funny. Second: most people are very self-conscious about their own noses. Most people hate them. Nose complexes abound. We told Sally Pardo that she had a noble nose and that dope began to screech like a barn owl. "That means too big, doesn't it? It means TOO BIG!" She just about went into paroxysms.

Everyone was dying to get a peek into our book but we were extremely cautious with it, conscious of its power. The schnozzola book was something like a package of TNT. It could cause fights, wars, suicides.

Still Tisha and I walked the corridors in constant study. When we passed people in the halls we'd let slip with the adjectives.

"Vinegar cruet."

"Phallic."

"Heaven bound."

"Common porker."

"Utilitarian."

"Abominable."

"Skewed."

Then we'd head into a quiet corner to enter these observations or add them to already extant entries. Nose entries were agglutinative. Some people already had a page and a half of nasal notes.

Alas, one day Toby Oberduerster grabbed the book. He ran into the study hall bellowing, "I GOT IT! I GOT THE NOSE BOOK!" Pandemonium ensued. A riot. Yelling boys. Screaming girls. Pages were snatched and ripped. Sally Pardo, that idiot, in hysterical tears as she read further elucidations on the nobility of her nose and failed to understand a word of it. Terry Hardcastle began punching right and left because Toby laughed at what the book said about her protuberance.

It was out of control until Ms Wilkins, who was both the Dean of Girls and our home Room teacher, stormed in like the U.S. Calvary. She captured the book and us.

When she got us in her office she said not a word. She plunked us into separate carrels on opposite sides of the room, then sent a monitor to the Home Ec Department to fetch two stand-up mirrors which she placed before us.

"Now look," she commanded.

"What are we supposed to be looking for?" Tisha asked. "Guess," replied Ms Wilkins.

BEYERDAHLS

UPSTANDING AS SENTINELS THE parents were, or seemed to be at first, but the Beyerdahls never were the luckiest family on this earth. For their first offspring they had Alfred who used to go down the evening streets of Brooklyn singing church hymns at the top of his register. You wouldn't believe how handsome that Alfred was. We girls adored him. He paid attention to us, too, little as we were, and that was rare. He was polite to little kids. That in itself should have alerted us to something radically wrong. Had we only experience enough, we'd have seen it. A school notebook of his once flew out the window of the high school bus. Right at my feet. I took it as a portent at the time. For years I saved that silly notebook in my treasure cache. We really mooned over Alfred until he started singing stuff down the length of 74th Street. We knew enough to be scared then. It was weirdness like he was warding something off. Everything. Desires and fears, maybe life itself, warding it all off by singing that church stuff as loud as his God would let him.

Joe was the second born, shy and quiet. He looked good enough too, but he soon started getting funny. He shot his BB's at our mother through the kitchen window. Mrs. Beyerdahl brought him around the next morning. She came dressed as if for a wedding, very formal, ominously quiet, almost too good-looking like all the Beyerdahls. Our mother was in shock because Mrs. Beyerdahl wasn't like anybody else on our block, not the kind to come calling. Ma had never even exchanged two words with the lady and Joe's mother really looked formidable to her, all dressed up with uncomfortable shoes, hose, even gloves and a hat. All our mother could do was keep wiping her hands on her apron. Mrs. Beyerdahl only said, "I think Joseph has something to say to you." He had to make an apology and he did it with all of us watching, maybe full of contrition, mumbling something nobody could possibly understand because it was mostly inaudible, and he told it all out while staring at his own big shoe. Ma had to stand still for this. Later she said, "Now he really gonna shoot me. His mama make him hate me." But I didn't think so. I thought it was only a waste of time because you could see the clown grin trying to surface, he was dying to laugh the whole time he was garbling out his words.

Joe got handsomer and handsomer but never as perfect looking as his brother Alfred. In puberty, though, he sort of started stealing stuff. Cars, mostly. He'd learned how to jump start them and would "borrow" them without asking, showing off to us kids. He got some kind of thrill out of it. Some of us thought he was a romantic figure, like a pirate or something. He'd always leave the cars when they ran out of gas, up someone's driveway or by a fireplug or somewhere where they weren't supposed to be. I wasn't totally turned off by him, either, because once when he was home from military school I saw him head into the schoolyard. My bedroom window looked right over Roosevelt schoolyard so I poked my freshly washed head out into the December blast. You could almost hear the pin curls in my hair crackling into ice as I watched Joe Beyerdahl trying to shoot baskets for hours. That night I dreamed he asked me to the prom at the Academy. The next morning I woke up with a cold that was about half an inch from pneumonia.

Cecil was the Beyerdahl's third kid. He was my age. Cecil seemed so nice and normal. He was the cute one. When we were little he played with us girls all the time. Whenever anyone got mad at him or wanted to make him toe the line he would make this funny sad face, stick his lower lip out, and then grin up in the cutest way. My sister Loretta just couldn't resist that grin. Cecil always got his way. He just used to remind us of a puppy that rolls over and shows you its soft belly. Our mother said it was the reason he was always playing with the girls, because they let him get away with murder, but I didn't think so. He just didn't like doing the stuff the boys wanted to do. Rough Maloneys ruled our street and Cecil hated getting hurt and hated getting dirty. He loved his neat clothes as much as he loved his own skin.

By the time we got to Roosevelt Junior High, Cecil was my best friend. He spent a lot of time with me, came over in the afternoon to do homework, looked for me in the halls, and told me all sorts of stuff. He said he was finding out about sex and, of course, what I knew wouldn't fill a teaspoon, so every little bit he shared I stashed in my pathetic collection of strange facts. Strange because all of it sounded mighty strange to me, almost impossible, like you could put it into **Believe It or Not**. Why would anyone want to do that? Aside from the embarrassment there were so many contortions involved. Cecil said all kinds of people did this stuff, even my parents, but I certainly didn't think so. Among other things they simply weren't nimble enough. But Cecil never mentioned his own family.

He never would talk about them though Loretta kept stringing him on, trying to get him to open up. Everybody in the neighborhood was dying to know what had happened to Alfred who had recently and totally disappeared from the block after a few years of assaulting our ears with baritone solos. The father had long ago vanished from sight: no one laid claim to having seen him for ages. Joe was back from the military school on a sick leave, the kids said. But I didn't think so. Booted out, I suspected. We could all see he'd started smoking funny stuff, something he shouldn't do. He held those butt ends like the hopheads did, and he looked spacey, always pleasant, a vague and lopsided grin always on him. Cecil didn't mention Joe. If someone remarked that Joe was home again about all he said was, "Oh, yeah."

Mrs. Beyerdahl became visibly pregnant, when she was visible, which was hardly ever. Details of things like this were off limits to us in those days, so we really had our eyes and ears open. I heard Pa comment to our mother, "Must have been an accident, Caterina." He had a funny look on his face. She gave the same look back at him and said, "The devil stirred the stew pot and forgot to put the lid back on!" Old world proverbs of that kind hopelessly confused my little stock of hard-won information about sex and babies though one thing I knew for certain, there would be no enlightenment from our little mother. She could be counted on to hang veils of mystery all around that particular subject. Once she told Loretta that she really didn't know for sure where babies came from, and once she told me that she got me by praying a lot.

Mrs. Beyerdahl's time finally came. We heard she had a girl. We didn't hear it from Cecil who never said a word on the subject. Mrs. Jacobskind told our mother that the baby was going to be called India,

23

only Mrs. J, who liked to put on a toney accent, sort of pronounced it "In-ja," so all of us started saying it that way except our mother who pronounced every vowel in her rolling Italian way. We were waiting to see if this new Beyerdahl was going to be as handsome as all the rest of them.

It was a Saturday when they brought her home. Mr. Beyerdahl had reappeared, kind of escorting the mother into the house. He was tall and unbending, just as we had first seen him when the Beyerdahls moved in. We were all sitting on the porch. Unexpectedly, Alfred stepped out of the cab with the new baby in his arms. Loretta nudged me so hard she almost knocked me off the porch. "See," she said triumphantly. She could never get over how good he looked. "He's all right now. I told you he was just drafted or on a trip or something."

Yeah, maybe. But I didn't think so. I thought he was probably out on a good-behavior from the looney bin.

Our parents, though, were really staring. They had strange looks on their faces. Pa said, "They look so much alike." He said it in a strange whispery voice, and very slowly.

"*Sembrano gemelli*, like twins," our mother agreed.

But none of that really registered with me because all I was thinking about was the baby, a cute little girl-child. I loved babies so much that I would play peek-a-boo for an hour, and I couldn't wait till In-ja would be outside and I could see her and play with her.

That didn't happen for a long time. Cecil still came around occasionally. He was totally silent about the baby. When you asked him how the baby was he'd change the subject real quick. New stuff was going on with Cecil now. He had started making these huge posters with modern swirling designs and wild colors. Miss Kratz, the art teacher, thought so much of them that she got him to make a series and they decorated the whole entry hall of Roosevelt Junior High with them. He gave them silly titles like LOVE OF AN AMOEBA FOR A PARAMECIUM or BORED OF EDUCATION. Kratz kept telling him they "aroused much positive comment," which Cecil would make fun of, imitating her ridiculous, flirty way of talking. Miss Kratz was still young and flapped her eyes at all the boys.

Even though he was only in junior high school, Cecil got himself a part in the church play. They were all adults in the group except for a couple of fat high school seniors that looked about as adult as anyone could in that company. Cecil was just a cute little boy. But when the play went on he was absolutely the best one in it. You could hear every word he said. When he came onstage the whole audience sat up as if charged by electricity, and he knew just what to do with their attention. People raved about him. They said he was practically a professional.

I saw less of him because he started going to a drama school in the city on Saturday mornings, but he still did come by. Only now when he came by all he could talk about was some guy named Lothar, who sounded absolutely boring. Lothar this and Lothar that. He said Lothar's name even when it had nothing to do with what we were talking about. "I don't even know Lothar," I said to Loretta, "but I'm already sick to death of him."

"It's only the beginning," she said in that smarty voice of hers that I hated so much.

"What do you mean?"

"You know, you really are some kind of dope, Connie," Loretta said. She was only a few years older than me and she thought she knew everything. "Haven't you even noticed that Cecil has started wearing eye makeup?"

Oh, I didn't think so. Cecil was just a very cute boy. He had those huge blue Beyerdahl eyes with the long black eyelashes. Talent had begun to ooze out of him so much that he shone.

As usual, we had no spring that year. One morning it turned from cold to hot and that was the morning we saw the pram in the Beyerdahl's driveway. Loretta and I were dying to go up to it but we were a little scared, too. The Beyerdahls were very private. They'd never been exactly welcoming to us kids. Loretta finally got up her nerve and she went over and looked in, then reared back again and backed up toward me. The look on her face was terrible. "Don't look, Connie!" she whispered.

"Why?"

"It's not a baby. It's a monster."

I looked anyway. In-ja had hair like the fluff of a chick's feathers. It wasn't real hair at all. Her skin was the white ceramic of a dish, but raked with scratches. You could see blood on fingernails like the translucent peelings of an onion, and far too long, untended. While I was looking at her she opened her mouth and began to bawl. It was a bloodcurdling cry, about a million decibels of it. The inside of her mouth was redder than blood. Even though only a few months old I could see she already had eyeteeth. That's all. Just those four little pointy dog's teeth in there. Unlike Loretta, I wasn't scared by this. I loved babies. I just felt so sorry for the poor kid. She looked just like a picture of an elves' changeling in my English Lit anthology, and the whole effect was only made worse by the presence of those deep, enormous, beautiful blue eyes that all the Beyerdahls shared. They were intelligent eyes, with a trace of epicanthic fold like some Scandinavians have, and they made her look wise, even wicked.

Just about then, Alfred slipped out of the shadows of the big ramshackle garage as if he'd been guarding from there all along, though he did nothing about her howling. "She has a condition," he announced.

"She also needs to be changed," I told him loftily.

He just slipped back into the shadows again.

"How do you like that?" Loretta asked me. "He's back home again."

But I didn't think so. Now I thought he'd been there all along, all those long months, lurking in the shadows of the garage or of the Beyerdahls' old frame house.

Of course, people noticed something wasn't right. In no time the whole block knew it. Mrs. Jacobskind clarified it. She was always the great source of information. Our mother, an open admirer of education, said Roberta Jacobskind had finished high school and even done a year of college. Mrs. J stopped over a lot. She loved the adulation our humble little mother gave her. For Mama, Roberta Jacobskind was the fountain of knowledge. She was the Eyes and Ears of the world. Interpreting everything. And she said the baby was born with a rare condition.

In-ja had hardly any pores in her skin. She could not perspire like a normal person. "Bad heredity," Mrs. Jacobskind declared importantly. She looked at our mother for about a minute after that. There was a nasty look on Mrs. J, I thought. Smug.

Well, it was true. The baby didn't sweat. It was now hot summertime and the pram was out in the driveway all day. You could hear In-ja howling most of the time. She had a screech worse than cats at night. We never saw anyone come out to tend her. Sometimes the hood of the pram would slide back and the kid would be baking out in the hot sun, just screaming. The heat made her nose bleed. Then she really looked like a fright, blood steaming down toward her gaping mouth, with the pointy little teeth showing, scratches all over her. I started going over to check if the hood was up. I'd take a wet washcloth. In-ja began to know me. She'd shut up screaming. She'd look at me and then at the rag, staring with those beautiful eyes. I won't say her look was an affectionate one, rather one of enormous curiosity, like, "What's all this with this face getting close to me with a cool rag and words?"

And words and words. I gave her words. It was no hardship for me, everyone knew I talked too much anyhow, and I figured In-ja needed to hear things. It certainly quieted her screaming. Her wizened little face would screw up attentively, as if she couldn't make out whether this stream of sound was dangerous or not.

Once when I was over there I saw Mrs. Beyerdahl at the window. I got scared because I thought she was watching me, maybe didn't like me fussing around her baby. But she wasn't looking at me. She was just staring. Staring empty. There was something terrible about those great blue eyes. They were looking at nothing and hopelessly seeing everything. Everything ugly and dreadful and inescapable and evil. Yet hers were the same huge, gorgeous, cerulean eyes that the baby had, and Alfred, and Joe, and Cecil and all of them.

Cecil's eyes were full of humor, only now even I had to admit he was putting make-up on them. Lots of it. It was so garish I couldn't pretend it wasn't there even though I still wanted to defend him against Loretta. She had gotten so she couldn't say a civil word about him, like she hated him. He came around less and less. He hardly mentioned Lothar anymore. If the name came up he made a prissy face. He started walking funny, swaying his behind. Loretta made note of that walk with scathing comments and our mother, who was in the room, just shrugged and said, "That's not nice, Loretta," but very softly, in an unconvinced way.

In Fall the schools started. It was hard on our street because we had the two schools, the parish elementary and the public junior high just across the street from it. When school let out hordes of children came streaming down, sometimes making pests of themselves.

In-ja was very precocious. They had her in a playpen now. She could stand and even totter a few steps, but always stuck in the driveway for the day. The kids found her and they'd gather around to say how ugly she was and make jokes and laugh at her. She looked like an imp from hell. Her hair was still a white fuzz. Her face was white too, dead white, and often caked with dried blood. She seemed to know the kids were inimical. She got mean as a hornet. She screamed all hell. They learned fast not to get too close. She raked them with her nasty nails. Once she bit a kid and I saw the awful punctured bite marks from those four canines. When I could, I'd go shoo off the kids. In-ja would quit screaming when she saw me, but she didn't exactly look friendly to me either. Mrs. Beyerdahl would be more and more often at that window. She didn't protect the baby at all. She didn't even seem to know In-ja was there. She just stared in that empty desolated way.

It went like that for a long time. Cecil and I got out of Roosevelt and went to different high schools. He never came around any more but I heard he was at Utrecht High making a spectacle of himself. They said he wore knickers, hand painted neckties so big they looked like flags, and that he let his hair grow down over his ears. Boys just didn't do stuff like that in those days. Even I was beginning to see a sinister meaning in it.

In-ja was wild now. From the minute she was big enough to climb out of the playpen she had started roaming the streets. No one stopped her. She'd aim toward the corners and pick fights with the bigger children. Now they stayed clear of her. Everybody knew In-ja. She was lethal. She ranged as far as Amsterdam Heights, which was practically the slums, where the kids were real hoodlums, and I guess she held her own even there because she came back alive. She looked dreadful. That look was usually enough to protect her. The fuzz on her head never grew into real hair. It was white and stuck out so she looked like a dandelion gone to seed. Her eyeteeth had grown. They were visible most of the time. She had not another tooth in her head. She kept those fingernails long and ragged. Some kind of weapon, I suppose.

Loretta said she saw her hanging around local bars. She said the men sometimes went out and gave her beer. Loretta wondered if they tried to touch her but I didn't think so. She didn't even look like a human. Once I spied her on the Parkway rifling garbage pails. Just a little kid rooting like a dog. It didn't surprise me too much. I never saw anyone feed her. When she spotted me, she moved away from the pail and let her arms hang down. She looked funny and mumbled something. I thought she might have said, "Hi," and that amazed me. Mostly she hated everybody. It could break your heart. All she got from people was their horrible or horrified reactions to her.

Even from our mother, who was usually kind. One day she staggered in looking hit. She said, "Costanza! Costanza!" and I came running. I could see she was shocked. "*Quel' mostro!*" she said indignantly. "That monster! Across the street. A piece of the devil!"

"What happened, Ma?"

"*Quella cosa...* INDIA! She chase me! She chase me from the corner!"

I couldn't help smirking. It was a funny picture. Our dignified little mother with the neat little bun at the back of her head, scampering home as if beset by the demon. And our mother softened. A smile played at the corner of her lips. But even while amused I suddenly felt such a wrenching pang of pity for the kid. "Ma," I said. "Nobody loves her. Nobody on God's earth."

"*Poverina!*" our mother said softly. Sadness immediately changed her face.

But the block was up in arms over the kid. She did anything. She cursed out the nuns from the parochial school when they took their afternoon stroll. She overturned the garbage pails. She threw rocks at the school children even when they had done nothing to her. She defecated on Zohmanns' front doorstep. The whole world was her enemy and no one knew what revenge she would take next, without check and without reprimand. The neighbors began taking their indignation to the Beyerdahls' door. They rang and rang and it frustrated them to new anger that no one answered even though they could see Mrs. Beyerdahl staring out the upstairs window. They would try going over there at night on the assumption that Mr. Beyerdahl might be home then, though no one had seen him since they brought In-ja home. Still there was no answer. And that went on for a while.

Then one evening all hell broke loose over there. It was a warm season again so most of the neighbors were out on their porches. We heard an enormous screeching. The Beyerdahls' front door smashed open. I mean, it almost came off its hinges, and Cecil tumbled out first. I hadn't seen him in quite a while. He was dressed in a woman's nightgown. He had something on his head that could have been a wig. And he was crying, sobbing loud, blubbering without caring who heard him. And behind him came Mrs. Beyerdahl with In-ja affixed to her arm. Mrs. Beyerdahl was dressed as she always was, as if she was going to a church tea, with hose and high heeled shoes. Her dress was kind of a formal print with a little peplum. But In-ja was attached to her, gripping hard, like a fury. All of her was in motion. You could hardly see the blur of her. She was screeching like a devil from hell, trying to destroy her mother. Kicking and ripping and biting. Even from across the street we could see that the woman's arms were covered with bleeding puncture wounds from those punishing teeth. It looked as if someone had taken an ice pick to her. She yelled mindlessly, "Where are you, Alfred? Where are you? In God's name, where are you? Look at her! Look at your baby! Come get your baby! Look at the baby you made!" She yelled that over and over.

In the instant you could feel electricity run over all those porches. People rose in revulsion and interest. I guess they called the police or something. Loretta and I didn't see it because our parents shepherded us inside. "Go upstairs," Papa ordered. As we were going up we heard him say to our mother, "Alfred! The son! *Che porcheria!*"

Ma just looked stricken. She looked sick. "*Povera creatura!*" she said weakly but we had no idea if she meant the poor creature was the mother or the child.

I was old enough now. They couldn't expect that I would be an innocent forever. I knew what they were thinking.

But I didn't think so.

I went up to my treasure cache. It was still in the back of the drawer. I pulled out the old notebook that had once flown out the window of the Fort Hamilton bus in the days when we all thought Alfred was a dreamboat. Those were happier times for the Beyerdahls, I suppose.

In the front cover of that tattered book, written with a broad point, was the proud inscription –

ALFRED THOMAS BEYERDAHL, JUNIOR.

If there was a junior there must have been a senior, I thought.

Alfred Thomas Beyerdahl Jr.

DISCOMBOBULATED

I swallowed the nerve pills Peter P. gave me and after some time I slipped over from the waking world to the shores of Lethe where Georgie B. awaited me. The first thing I saw was his name.

Everywhere.

It was written in the firmament. It was spelled out in stars. I saw it pressed into the paving stones of the sidewalks of the nether world. BIFF, it said.

Placards broadcast it all over the supermarkets of hell.

BIFF was everywhere. BIFF. BIFFY. Bargain BIFF available here. SuperBIFF. Buy two BIFFS, get three.

On the handwritten menu at Bembo's restaurant I saw BIFFsteak, BIFFstew, BIFFalfredo, marinade of BIFF. Luisa Bembo was writing out the new menu cars for tomorrow. She pasted little icons on the four corners of the page. They were beige diamond stickers with a little red flame on them. "What's that, Lou?" I asked.

"It stands for the BIFFination," she said, looking dreamy, half enamored.

"What is BIFF?"

"I am," Georgie interrupted. "I am BIFF," he said in that smarmy voice he had, like a 1940's radio announcer.

"For crying out loud, Georgie," I protested. "It's practically sacrilege to say that!"

"Well, don't get BIFFy about it. It's only the truth. My name."

That's so. Georgie BIFF. "But it isn't the same thing at all," I argued.

Georgie got offended. Confused, too. His identity was leaking away into signboards, street signs, headlines, bus stops, tee shirts. It wasn't leaving him much BIFFery of his own.

A skywriter passed overhead. It wrote BIFF BIFF BIFF. three times, but as it traced the second the first was beginning to disperse and, by the time it wrote the third, the first was nothing but shreds of BIFFy puffs.

I was worried about Georgie, so I whisked him into a cab and we headed down Highway 66 at a fast clip. There was a fat truck in front of us and our driver wanted to pass him. Every time the cabby veered left to pass, the truck swerved out. "He's doing that on purpose!" I cried. The nerve! To add insult, on the back of the truck it said, HOW'S MY DRIVING? CALL 243 2433.

Georgie grabbed my cell phone. "I'm going to report him!" he announced but when he dialed he turned pale. "Do you realize what these numbers spell?"

2433

2433

And then, with the receiver to his ear, he began to tremble. I grabbed the phone out of his hand. "BIFFogenies recapitulates BIFFographies," said a portentous voice, over and over, and, with each repetition of the phrase, Georgie B. was slowly dematerializing.

I could do nothing but retrace my steps, back to the world you live in.

Peter P. was waiting. His eyes were staring. I could see he was sorely troubled. "Look at your hat," he said in a choking voice.

I had on a little dinkum hat with a beak. On the band it said POPP.

POPP. POPP was written on all the magazines on the coffee table. The letters on the espresso machine spelled **POPP**erino.

The radio interrupted the **POPP**ibel Cannon to say, "A **POPP** a day keeps the devil away," and "In **POPP**ery there is strength."

My mother called out from the other room. "Stay for dinner, Peter dear," she said. "We're having **POPP**chops. Afterward we can play some **POPP**er."

"I can't go through this again," I groaned.

Peter **POPP** ran out the door. Then he doubled back in. "Look out here," he called. "This should interest you." On the doorsill sat a huge package. It was addressed to **BACC.** I began to grow apprehensive. The neighbors' duck flew up on to the fence. "**BACC**," it cried, "**BACC! BACC! BACCA! BACCARO!**"

"That's me!"

I started to dematerialize. My mother called me, "**BACC!**"

But it was no use. Once I started this bizarre story there was no way of going **BACC**.

AN ANTIC DISPOSITION

ELIZABETH CUFFEE IS DEAD.

A stranger called Thursday night. He said, "Your name was in one of my mother's old address books. She's dead." Just like that. It was like a slap; I didn't even know of whom he was speaking.

"Who? Who? Who is this? Who died?"

"Lovander, Betty Lovander," he replied, and then he hung up.

I sat a moment reflecting on the rudeness of the speaker. For a moment I felt personally affronted by it. No one has manners anymore. Upon considered reflection, however, I decided to forgive him. Here was a fellow announcing a death; the death of his mother no less. A brusque expression was to be excused.

Then I began mentally picking at the message. Who? Betty Lovander. Betty Lovander. Working Betty Lovander up. I couldn't remember any Betty. Maybe Lovander could bring up something. It did awaken a negative buzz in my head, a disagreeable hum of familiarity, but it was a wraith that just teased the edges of my memory. So who could Betty Lovander be? She'd known me. I had appeared in one of her old address books. How old? Why didn't I ask him? But you can hardly ask anything of people like that. Rudeness is a banner too many people flaunt nowadays.

So Betty. Betty... Betty. Betty swam back, kept swimming by, unrecognized. Then it came to me. Doesn't Betty result from Elizabeth sometimes? Elizabeth!

Elizabeth Cuffee! Lizzie! It sprang into my mind. And Lovander too. Yes, there was a Lovander back there somewhere. Up my street. Harold, I think. Unpleasant fellow. Unpleasant remarks. A word. *Expunged.* If I

36

tried I could almost remember the remark he made. He was handsome. He thought so. Lizzie Cuffee thought so too. She had a crush on him way back then, way back, way *way* back in a distant existence that now floated up so readily.

It had been at least fifty years since I had heard or even thought of Elizabeth Cuffee. Now the past crowded in as if yesterday. The news of her death was affecting me deeply. Lizzie had been my boon companion at an age when girls are insufferable and need a bosom pal to be obnoxious with. We were that kind of silly girls together once, inseparable. We went through the crazy years together. Too old to be children and too young to be teenagers.

In the evening when the heat was down, Elizabeth and I sat on the front porch of the Cuffee house. We were writing a musical comedy which we had no doubt would storm Broadway and then, ultimately, the films. We even had the temerity to cast it. In the scene we were reworking for about the eleventh time there was a doctor, played by Gregory Peck, and a nurse played by Zazu Pitts or me, or Lizzie Cuffee for the wildest interpretation, as only Lizzie could be wild. A man came into the scene, maybe Edwin O'Brien or some actor of that rough but handsome ilk. Limping. The nurse, who was me sometimes and sometimes Lizzie Cuffee, said, "What's the matter, Mister?" and the man replied, "Sis, I've got a blister." This transmuted into a glorious song, lively and melodious when the two of us were not too much handicapped by giggles. Before long it became a Hollywood extravaganza as the backdrop rose to display the alley behind the doctor's office wherein three garbage cans did an elaborate tap dance routine while punctuating the rhythm with timpani from the lids. This cracked us up.

We were actually laughing when, all of a sudden, there came a ray of refracted light which distorted our reality. At first everything was turned into night. People passing on the street, even the blonde Norwegians who were walking down to the Norske Tidende office on Third Avenue became Negroes. After the first shock of change we realized that we were shrinking. I stood in my bare naked skin, climbing over my own clothes. I could hear mortal cries coming out of Lizzie Cuffee's shoe. Elizabeth Cuffee had shrunk down right into her own sock. I heard her muffled sounds as she struggled out of the cloth. The shoe began to rock. So great was her strength that she tumbled the shoe sideways and

I saw her crawl out. It was terrible. For a long time we looked at each other silently. I was still standing, naked, in one of my penny loafers The seriousness of the situation was beginning to dawn on us.

"What happened?" I asked.

"I think it is an alien ray coming in from outer space. I read about something like that in Astounding Tales once."

"I'm freezing," I complained. "Why us? Why are they picking on us?"

"Maybe it's not only just us," Lizzie said.

"Everyone shrunk?" I said. "Do you think this happened to everyone?"

"Makes sense," said Lizzie Cuffee. "On this planet all forms of life are based on the carbon molecule. Probably everything is affected." Elizabeth Cuffee was so smart, much smarter than I was.

"Everything?"

"Every living thing."

"Even my mother and father?"

"*Especially* your mother and father," she decreed with just a hint of malice. So darn smart, she was. "Think of the advantages," Lizzie said "We're tiny now like little mice."

"What's so great about that?" I complained.

"It's great for our spy business. We can slip around. We can watch people. We can be spies." She was still grappling with the vast mass of her thick, klutzy sock. At least it covered her nakedness.

"How can we spy on people if everyone else is mouse size too?"

"Oh, right," Lizzie replied. "Must be great for something though."

I was beginning to like standing by my shoe on Cuffee's front porch. I felt as if I was near the prow of a little boat, a rowboat of some kind. I didn't like being naked out there though.

Cuffees lived next door, much to my mother's chagrin. She couldn't stand them and she didn't like Elizabeth much either. "They all have those thick Brooklyn accents," Mama complained, which was kind of silly because we did live in Brooklyn, didn't we, and probably had the same accent anyhow. "You could pick a friend with more manners," she said though I couldn't imagine Lizzie being less than polite to her since she, Lizzie, always avoided any confrontation with either of my parents. She hid. Was that impolite? I did the same to avoid confrontation with all adults at that stage of my life. I really believed it was not because of manners but because of the way Elizabeth Cuffee looked.

She was ugly. She had an idiot's face. Her teeth climbed over one another. The way she wore her hair only accentuated the fact that her skull was misshapen. Her eyes were big and green but far too close together. She had breathing problems that caused her to hang her mouth open more than was normal or attractive, signaling abysmal stupidity. Frequently her nose was running and she was usually too busy to wipe it. But Lizzie was in actuality a kind of neighborhood genius. Only kids knew that. Adults took her at face value which, in her case, was less than zero.

I liked her a lot. She could dream up the most fantastic scenarios for games. That's what she called our imagination games, *scenarios.* Lizzie had the most intricate vocabulary. She had the best words for almost everything. *Scenario* was a word she had learned from the movie magazines. She read movie magazines voraciously. She was enamored of everything Hollywood and she knew all about the stars, as much as could be gleaned from the movie magazines of that era which dealt in flattery and the elaborate whitewashing of facts. Lizzie was so funny, too. She had me doubled up with laughter when she got started. "You could be on the radio, Lizzie, You are so funny." Once she replied, "I know. But it's just that I have an antic disposition." It was expressions like "an antic disposition" that kept me coming back for more. She had a walloping big vocabulary and she knew how to use it for fun and insult. Insult was important in those days. Girls got big hates on one another and the only thing that could shut them up was a powerful enough insult to counter theirs. It was not fashionable to use bad words in those days. I was not adept at the cross-derogatory play so Lizzie would protect me. She didn't even shy at saying "Bitch!" when necessary. A word like that was like a volcanic bomb. It scared most of us to death but not Lizzie.

That Lovander kid knew words, too. Once he called me a swot. I didn't even know what that meant. Lizzie came to my defense but Lovander topped her. He said, "You're even more of a swot, you and your mouthful of teeth. Lizzie Cuffee. Ugliness like yours can never be expunged," and she began to cry. "Expunged," he said. I guess she cried because she liked him and he was the first boy she ever liked.

Later she confided in me. "I'm going to get him to love me," she said.

"How?"

"If I can get him to laugh I can get him to love me," she explained.

Crazy, but I believed it. She could be so clever and so funny. Once we were in trouble at school, it all came back now, laughing uncontrollably at some moment when we were supposed to be solemn, Mr. Bloom pulled us out of the assembly. Bloom was the dean of boys, supposed to be an ogre. He was going to throw the book at us for this silly infraction of the rules. "Young ladies, what, may I ask, was so funny?"

Lizzie handed him a sheet of paper. He looked. He began to laugh until he almost choked. When he was all out of breath he gasped, "Go to your classes now. Go!"

"What the heck was on that sheet of paper?" I asked her.

"Just a cartoon I drew of Mrs. Murdock." Lizzie's cartoons could be devastating. I guess Bloom didn't like Mrs. M. much.

She was once my boon companion. I wonder what happened to Lizzie. So many years ago. I wished I knew more of her story. Wished I knew when Lovander came into it. Did she make him laugh? I wish I'd kept up with her. She was so special. She had an antic disposition.

I grieve for that child.

Lizzy Cuffee is dead.

DATING AND MATING IN MANHATTAN

(a chapter from a novel in progress)

IN LATE SUMMER MARY Ellen Rigg came to visit Jess. She looked like a heroine from a gothic novel, careless curls trained to frame her cameo face. It surely took a precious hour of each day to arrange this careless style, Jess reflected. Not to mention the makeup. Careful application of colors to the eyes gave her a semblance of wide-eyed innocence though something, the bridge of the nose, perhaps, too high, too haughty, suggested something different. From that face, which somewhat resembled a duchess imitating a little girl, rings of smoke now issued.

In unexpected combinations, Mary Ellen was growing more beautiful since their shared college days. Though they had exchanged some lively phone calls, Jess had not seen her since graduation and could see now that at last she was beginning to fit her face. Her occasional smile disclosed great healthy horse teeth, very dazzling. Her deep eyes changed shades with the shifts in her interior climate. Now that the summer had scorched her cheeks, her eyes appeared green. She was like a wild tribal princess, invincible yet wearing a style of Jane Eyre ringlets that pulled attention to the line of her neck, to the vulnerability of her throat. Flaunting a kind of innocence, which was a joke. Jessy knew Mary Ellen had given her innocence up several romances ago. Nevertheless, an idiotic sort of faith in romance prevailed.

Mary Ellen used to laugh a lot. In the old days, she did. But Jess remembered more than that. She remembered one of Mary Ellen's stunts, observed all those years ago. This was the memory: Mary Ellen grabbed Frank's hand, tugged at it as if to urge him up. But Frank couldn't move because Jess didn't, so he sat in an awkward stupor. And Mary Ellen kept his hand. Dreamily she played with his fingers. Frank's face was dopey, wondering what she was doing. He didn't have a clue, the big dope. Well, Jess could see Mary Ellen was working a little seduction on her boyfriend and right in front of her! Frank was too polite to snatch his hand away. The whole scene would have been funny if there had not been a subtle taint of treachery to it. But that was years ago.

Now, they were sitting in the late afternoon light in the little kitchen of Jessy's New York apartment. Jess was marveling at Mary Ellen's look, glowering, emitting anger in rings of smoke. Her friend's pellucid skin gave up shades of russet as interior tides, angers, raged under her sunburn, illuminating her like the chimney of a lamp that guards its flame from the wind. Her chin, noble in displeasure, lifted haughtily. "You've got Frank, Jessica. You can't imagine what it's like. I mean it. A jungle. I mean, with seven girls to every man…

"The parties, Jessy. They're certainly not for fun any more. They don't even pretend to be fun. They're predatory. Nobody dreams of liking anyone else. Guys actually cruise by girls and say, 'Do you screw?' They want a one-word answer. If it's 'no' they keep right on cruising, hardly breaking stride, passing out the same question to the next girl, not even bothering to rephrase it. The first time I heard that question I got ready to slap a face but the guy was gone even as I was winding up. I mean, kiddo, they want a *fast* answer, spelled Y-E-S, or they just scurry along.

"I was appalled. I even told Tony about it. You remember that Tony Baloney? The guy who wouldn't pay back the ten bucks he borrowed to take <u>me</u> home in a taxi? Light as a butterfly, alas. Anyhow, Tony knew exactly what I was talking about. 'An established technique,' he said. 'The Buckshot Approach. Spread your bullets. A real time saver,' Tony assured me. At a party of any size you're bound to find at least a handful of girls who <u>will</u> screw without preamble.

"Can you imagine, Jess? Can you imagine any girl answering 'yes' to that proposition? Yet it must be true. And then what happens to the subtleties, to all those intriguing preliminaries and nuances that make a love story out of the same old unvarying reproductive impetus?

"Tony Baloney told me off," Mary Ellen said, now switching to a rough street voice, "'Who has time for all that shit? You must be stupid or something. Where do you come from anyway?' Oh, Tony's really a charmer, a real gift with words. I've got the colorful characters for neighbors. My building is beginning to seem like a haven for life's misfits. I mean, aside from fairy princesses like Tony Baloney, who is satisfied with your money, everybody you meet wants to lay you flat at once with a minimum interference of words. A simple 'yes' is all the conversation they can handle – or else they present you with some kink that temporarily unbalances your understanding. At least the special interest guys converse. It takes a little explanation to communicate special requests. Like this guy I met at a bar on Fire Island. A real truck driver type, a bruiser. He worked up a sweat trying to be charming. Finally he made his pitch, a request that I go to bed with his boyfriend. Boyfriend was this little squinchy guy with a huge head and a tiny almost unformed body. He scuttled around the bar frantically, but never took his insect eyes off me while boyfriend made his case. Can you believe it, Jessy? They just liked to watch each other he said. The amazing part – I actually felt sorry for the two of them. Imagine explaining your kinky thing over and over again, what must that be like?

"That same evening I met a guy who looked to have jumped out of one of those health catalogs. Mr. Perfect. Everything he had on was plaid, even the band of his wristwatch. He kept nudging me to go off to some party. I was about to go, too, anything preferable to the present snake pit. I mean, I could imagine what it would be like. While he talked to me, his eyes smeared over every other girl in the room. About then one of the bungalow belles, it was Loris, I think, came over, laughing her head off. 'I see you met Milton the Merman,' she said. She told me that his specialty was dragging girls to this decaying mansion in Ocean Bluffs where everyone goes skinny-dipping. They wouldn't let him in unless he brought a girl. That was all that Milton ever did-skinny dip and look around. ''There's something wrong with him,' Loris said. 'He doesn't even have a normal reaction, if you know what I mean. It's more like a dirty little boy kind of thing.'

"I asked her if she'd ever accepted his invitation but either she didn't hear me or used the bar noise to make believe she didn't. Well, I just wanted to ask her if his underwear was plaid, too. But that Loris is a real mixed-up girl, anyhow. She tells you all kind of personal junk you don't even want to hear, but if you ask a question she gets very huffy, very mind-your-own-businessy.

"We both gave up on the bar early that night and walked back to the bungalow together. I told her about the Buckshot Approach. She'd heard it all before, of course. She said, 'You know something? It <u>always</u> works.' She thought the big guy propositioning me on behalf of his boyfriend was a really amusing anecdote. 'Lucky you,' she said, 'you really had a fun evening.' I couldn't tell if she was being sarcastic or what. Then she got real quiet, walking and looking at the moon. Suddenly she stopped, grabbed my arm. 'Hey, I know what! Let's rent a sand buggy and go down to Cherry Grove to look at the queers!'

"I mean, Jess, don't you think that's sick? The whole crew at that bungalow is deranged. Everyone hates every one else. They're all down there for just one reason – to snag a man. Don't look at me funny. I know. I'm included.

"Dodie Kraminosky brought in two other shareholders– Loris and Doris, or Lusitania and Catatonia. Some such thing. I don't know. I mean, I 'm sharing a summer beach cottage with these girls and I don't even know their names. That's just the way it is. Buckshot, buckshot everywhere.

"Dodie has this boyfriend out there – Joel. He weighs about 350 pounds and he had no eyes, just these bloops of glass riding his cheeks and below that a pair of lips that look like the spreader on a mucilage bottle. He sprays when he talks. Gases issue out of him when he walks. None of that matters. Dodie is mad for him. She has fits of hysteria when he points his glass bloops at another girl; —and he does point, not just his glasses, either. She threw a tantrum one night at the Bayview Bar because he wouldn't hang with her. About six people rushed in to help. They thought she was having an epileptic seizure. Joel was imperturbable. He'd have cheerfully let her roll around in the sawdust all evening. He loved that. She's desperate to hold on to the creep and Dodie is even a rather pretty girl, Jessie. But with mean eyes. Squinty.

"Joan came in as a visitor. She brought a bag of peaches. She figured that meant she could stay the weekend without sharing in any expenses. She is a moocher genius. She is also an artful predator with snares out in every direction. She snared a little boy from Joel's cottage. This little

Arnie has lost his soul to her. He's like a happy robot. He can be made to empty the garbage, scour the toilet, fight a war, scale Everest – anything to hang at our place near Joanie.

"She is so solicitous of him, so helpless around him, so totally uninformed. You forget that she actually has her master's degree in microbiology. He knows that, so it flatters his soul when she acts like the tiniest kernel of information he coughs up is a revelation. With her incredibly idiotic look of sweet myopia, she leans on him for wisdom and protection. You remember that ploy, Jess? It means she can tease like hell but he is not supposed to touch her. She unburdens her little girlie troubles on him. He's a field of ears; I mean, I think he is growing an extra pair of ears on the sides of his nose the better to hear her.

"She tells him how everyone was mad at her because she had not coughed up a share of the cottage expense – remember the bag of peaches? I've gotta tell you, Joanie is so cheap she had the nerve to ask Loris for gas money for a fifteen minute lift she gave her to the ferry station. Well, she made some story about how Loris had skunked and dissed her. Arnie, with all of his thousand ears twitching, tries to warn her about these false friends that surround her, and she just blinks and says, 'Don't say that, Arnie. It isn't worthy of you!'

"Really, she's a virtuoso.

"On a weekend she came with her bag of produce and Maria. Maria is a friend of hers, pregnant, big as a whale. A real scatty girl. Doris asked her who the daddy was and Maria said, 'I don't know. It's a real small ship that knows who's aboard.' Would you believe? She came out to hit the bar scene with Joan. She said, 'I may have missed the boat, but I'll be damned if I'm gonna get off the pier.' Very nautical.

"Joanie informed Arnie that he had to help her entertain Maria for the evening, for she could not bear to think of Maria pining away alone. While she said this Maria was sitting in front of the big theatrical, illuminated make-up mirror that belongs to one of the other maidens, preening herself for an evening that didn't take Arnie or Joanie into account at all. Arnie agreed to baby-sit. He'll do anything Joan asks. So there Arnie sat obediently while Joan went off to the lists. She left him there with Maria, who soon went bar hopping just as Joanie had.

"There's such a doggy feeling to all this. I think back to school and it seems to me there used to be some attempt to be friends. I mean, really try to like each other, like with Chooky Linkus. I can't remember why I was so down on him. He was always trying to be a friend of mine."

"I had a letter from Lucy Chadwick," Jess replied. "She says Chooky is in Chicago. Just went through a messy divorce. You know he was always so crazy about you, Mary Ellen. And you treated him like dirt."

"Oh, Lucy. I've lost touch with Lucy. Can you get me her phone number?" So replied Mary Ellen, leaning way back, her green eyes gazing in another direction. She could look like a portrait musing at you from the walls of an elegant gallery – a great lady immortalized in her greatest moment, surrounded by dross, nevertheless a queen.

Mary Ellen leaned away and, looking elsewhere, letting slide off her the smutch of recent experiences.

Katherine Baccaro

THE CENSUS

AFTER THE SLIGHT RAIN the street was veiled with Turkish mud like the slip that potters work clay with. Linda, in a foul mood, was terrified of sliding. This whole voyage with the Golden Argonauts had suddenly made her too conscious of her age. Nimbleness and the quicker attributes were fading. Even under better circumstances she knew her balance was treacherous. Her imagination foretold what it would be like for her feet to fly forward, plopping the seat of her light linen skirt into the abominable gunk. Ludicrous. It wasn't dirt or pain she feared, but the embarrassment, both hers and Sterling's, and the solicitousness of strangers.

Yesterday, visiting Wooley's digs on the Amuq plain, one of the men with the group had slid halfway down the rubble into the ruins of a bronze age temple ("or palace, or granary, difficult to say for certain," their archeologist had explained.) That man became gruff, almost angry. Half a dozen clucking women descended. The other men just glanced with deliberately blanked eyes. "Nothing! It's nothing!" he barked at the little flock, flapping them away with an arm. They hesitated, convinced it probably *was* something. There must be a bruise, a lacerated spot secretly leaking blood under the leg of his trousers. But he refused to share. A tall woman standing clear of the incident said, "Falling is terribly embarrassing for some reason. When tourism began in China the government had to warn the people not to laugh if foreigners slipped or fell. A face-saving thing, you know, that laughter." Linda stared at the woman. She had a flat accent and her words flew flat as frisbees flung out of a mouthful of huge, aggressive looking teeth. Of course, Sterling rose to the occasion. "Sure," he said. "It's like saying, 'I know you didn't really fall. You were just kidding around.' And the government ain't gonna stop them from laughing, I'll tell you that. They laughed the first time I went to China, when it first had opened up for tourists, and they were still laughing, laughing and spitting too, for that matter, last autumn." The woman just looked noncommittal and pulled her lips back over her large teeth. Sterling practically hummed. Pleased. It was something like a cat purring, Linda thought. She knew he never ceased to marvel at the amount of good stuff he kept finding tucked away in his cerebellum.

The whole hokey excursion had been his idea, a jolt for the brain of which he was so proud. To Linda it seemed the poor archeologist must suffer. She was explaining rock piles to people who were incapable of seeing in them the street plan of ancient Alalakh, even though they clustered around emitting gasps of wonder and staring at everything. Linda saw one man intently examining an ant hill. Perhaps he was an entomologist, but she didn't think so. Had there been a fire hydrant in the rubble, would he have studied it?

Everywhere the archeologist went she was shagged by the main body of the group, all expecting instant enlightenment. Dr. Harcourt-Styne. No first name or short name offered. Looking threatened, looking not used to this sort of expedition at all. Sometimes when she stopped the whole group surged up on her, she seemed trapped as if she had absolutely nothing to say, or only typical travelers' words like, "If we don't find a toilet soon I'll…" Some of the comments she made were obscure. Linda kept a distance away, disturbed by references to Seluccids, Seljuks, Marmalukes, peoples she couldn't quite believe in, never having heard of them before.

They stayed in Antarkia, ancient Antioch, to see the few remaining Christian sites and the museum that had a head of the Bronze Age king whose city they'd so recently stumbled through. Tolerant mosques guarded Christian relics on all sides. They had to file through a primitive toilet. There was nothing else around. Linda and Sterling waited outside. He said, "Notice how some of these local men come out of there and just keep eternally fingering themselves? Those baggy pants can't require all that much adjustment. Excessive stimulation of their own equipment, I calls it." Was she supposed to smile? She looked, instead, at the Great Man. Likenesses of the Great Man were everywhere, depicted on the sides of buildings, on flags, posted in every shop and lobby. She'd seen him replicated in an ice block at a fancy restaurant, outlined in tessera, in stone, in wire, in gravel, even in cinders and on the tiles of the paving blocks. In full or half or three quarter face, or profile, always recognizable, always the Great Man. "He must have been something," she mused. "They're still venerating him fifty years later."

"Remember the monument to Chiang in Taiwan?" Sterling said. But it wasn't the same thing at all.

Then the census surprised them. No one seemed to have known about it. Not even Doll Hartmann, the toothy woman. The management said they'd have to be confined to the hotel all of the next day while the Turks went about the business of counting themselves. Dr. Harcourt-Styne could only blink. Doll let her teeth hang out unattended. They all sat at the long table in a state of mild shock. Sterling started clearing his throat. Linda cringed in anticipation. Quite suddenly he turned to the waiter standing behind him. "SHUT UP!" he shouted. That was what they all heard. Everybody looked embarrassed. But the young waiter smiled and took off while Sterling grinned. He was humming again. "It's wonderful to know only a few words in a language," he said. "I say something and maybe it turns out it ain't what I think I said. Now let's see what that guy's gonna do." Humming a mile a minute. This business with the grammatical slips and colloquialisms was something new, perhaps a cuteness he was cultivating for his imminent old age.

The waiter came sailing back, smiling, bearing bottles of Turkish wine. Sterling held it up. "SHARAP!" he announced with a twinkle. Owens, the man who had barked his shin, actually applauded, and Sterling laughed a laugh of genuine happiness. It awakened a memory. So many times that laugh had gladdened her heart. He laughed like that when he first appeared, an unknown young man who showed up at the girls' dorm, bringing history notes that in her distracted way she had left somewhere. "You saved me," she had said. "These notes are the frail link between me and the rest of my career!" He laughed. He used to laugh whenever he thought he had pleased her. And now as she looked at him the years seemed to slip off his face. It firmed up sharp and bright. She could once more see the happy boy under the eroding flesh.

So long ago, that business with the history notes, almost as long ago as Ataturk.

"You mean to tell me that they intend to do in one day what the United States takes a year to do?" Owens' wife remarked. She was an elegant lady, round eyed, perpetually surprised expression. The variety, color and draping of her clothes had kept the women buzzing in the three hectic days since Linda and Sterling had joined the group. She entered a room in stages. First she would tilt her body languidly, slant it. Cock the leading arm against her hip, survey the room with those round eyes. The thin-lipped almost humorless smile capped off her astonished air, as if she were announcing something ridiculous, like, "Would you believe that this is what's become of me?" She pushed her head forward, looked at everyone through the top of her eyes. For a moment Linda thought she saw the intense young woman this had surely once been.

"Well, as a matter of fact," Harcourt-Styne said hesitantly, "I just read an apparently well-intentioned article that claimed a small cadre of Malthusian experts with a few properly trained technicians could have conducted our census with equally accurate—or even more accurate—results."

"Not surprising. Not surprising," Owens remarked gruffly. "Seems to me we do everything in the most wasteful, extravagant, and least efficient way these days. We did better once."

"He was always an optimist. Not me. Never. I was the protester," his wife said. Her smile coupled with the surprised look made her seem a child caught at some minor transgression. "I was a Hippy," she admitted. "One of the first." And Owens leaned back in his chair, eyeing the company at large with deep personal satisfaction. His wife's history of protest seemed to round him out.

"I was before that," Doll admitted, her laugh erupting like a giggle. "A Bohemian when Hippy was a cruel description or a nickname for a large zoo animal." Suddenly Linda saw her, too. In those great white teeth she could see the focus of a smile that might have lighted up the hearts of shaggy young poets sitting in the unheated spaces of Village lofts. "I bet you were the inspiration for poetry once," Linda blurted out. Doll looked a little bit startled. Then she loosed her big smile again. "And I'll bet you were the one who needed to make everyone feel good, the one who jostled people into happiness," Doll retorted.

"No. That was Sterling," Linda said. And out of the corner of her eye she could see he was revving up again, humming, purring. He hadn't changed. What she had once loved him for was still there. As Linda's gaze traveled down the long table all the elderly and middle-aged Argonaut faces began to shed their years for her. Harcourt-Styne in the intensity with which she listened to the man next to her seemed to be displaying a receptiveness, the innocence of enduring intellectual curiosity. Linda realized that Owens and his wife must be her own contemporaries, and she could see him, a positive and earnest young man escorting that round-eyed girl whose sights were firmly fixed on righting some wrong. Mrs. Owens had probably worn a braid down her back, Linda thought. Maybe a band around her forehead. Years slid off. The sparkle returned to tired eyes. Chins were firm again. They addressed each other with affection, as if they were about to make friends for a long future. Perhaps it was the wine, though Linda had found it rough and hardly touched it.

At six of the next evening the Turkish census was ended and they could board the bus to continue their journey. Outside the hotel door the Orantes flowed, trapped there in its ancient embankments. It was already growing darker. Autumn. She grabbed Sterling's hand. He laughed, perhaps to save her face, but she understood that to be a matter of her own interpretation. She drew him to their seats and began looking fixedly out the window of the bus.

A sliver of moon was hooking a single star, but the crescent of it seemed even thinner than the one on the red flag, thin as a wire, like a curved crack of light in the dark sky.

RESTORATION COMEDY

I DIED IN THE accident.

With whirrs and beeps and penetrating lights the Committee reconstituted the scrambled parts that lay on the table before them. In the cavity that was the skull invading sensors detected a mass which was immediately activated by electrical impetus. Similarly a lump that was the dead heart was kick-started into motion. It pumped. The new action of the brain inaugurated a series of synapses along pathways of the nerves. They raced through the corpus, tipping into a thousand minute junctures, until a whole new system was ignited. And the heart's new movement inspired a river of the blood, but it was not my blood. My blood had long since flaked off into the wind, or seeped into the fabric of the tarmac. The same amazing technology that was responsible for the whirring and flashing of numerous invasive life-saving devices had devised a new artificial fluid. Hematostretz, they called it. Ersatz blood.

So it was that I came to consciousness, if not to life, the cynosure of many interested eyes. I was surrounded by teams of renowned genius, innovators who thrilled to see the results of their inventions now animating my limbs and spurring to attention my life signs. I exhibited a pulse and blood pressure and temperature.

They asked me questions only to see if I could talk, and I could.

"How do you feel?" they asked.

"Okay," I replied because to say "Good" would have been an indication of quality whereas Okay was merely an assent to the question. I did feel however, though the quality of the feeling was beyond the possibility of description. Neither pain nor pleasure disturbed my constructed existence. Manipulations were pressed upon my surface, apparently intended to induce sensations. Vast areas of my superficies were covered by a new porous plastic that was said to breathe, that is to say, vital gases transpired to and from my interior. They called this wondrous pellicle Dermavitae.

I was continuously attended by a convocation of learned scientists who vied to provoke reactions from my inert body. Any reaction rewarded them. On one occasion a rupture in the Dermavitae caused an opening, permitting a trickle of precious Hematostretz to ooze out. The doctors fluttered about in various stages of delight though the leak could have ended all their good postulations. After ascertaining that some offending Novossum, the bone substitute that comprised my frame work, had glitched and caused the unfortunate diduction, the scholarly doctors were hesitant to seal the aperture. There was so much to be learned from even such an unfortunate incident. Could Hematostretz, close as it was to a reproduction of human blood, coagulate? Was Dermavitae, like cellular skin, capable of healing itself, and would some equivalent of scar tissue result? And, if it did, could it in any way compromise the integrity of the whole? How long would any potential regeneration take? If the framework was so unpredictable could more such shocking errata be anticipated?

The matter of my nourishment became a pressing problem as it was discovered that, though my flesh was surrogate, my cells did grow. Key nutritionists laboring with microcellular consultants and top-flight mechanics finally devised a substance consisting of soy syrup and vegetable fiber suspended in a mineral gel. Small amounts were introduced in the Pseudogastrum using intercalation techniques. At first the Committee was baffled at the absence of any waste though, amid much laughter, they assured each other that I had the apparatus for evacuation. At last it was discovered that the Dermavitae had the marvelous property of transpiring superfluous gases from the body and into the surrounding air. For this reason most of the scientists found it difficult to stay near me for long periods of time.

Except for Dr. E.Z. Dr. E.Z. thrived on my exhalations.

Foremost among the gathered pundits was Dr. Elizabeth Zerjieff to whom all the others deferred. Dr. Zerjieff had apparently been a pioneer in the development of both Hematostretz and Dermavitae.

She took no credit for the invention of Novossum. In fact she deplored the recent malfunction and was openly critical of its makers. It had been her idea to put these and other medical innovations to use in the reconstruction of an actual life form so if others were less than perfect in their scientific applications it stood fair to ruin her conception of the New Being, Essenovum, which was me, the Restoration. I was her baby, as some of the scientists liked to say. One of the doctors remarked, "She was determined to change some clutter into her creature." Dr. Zerjieff heard about that and was very angry. She said it was an unkind observation and should not have been made within my hearing though it meant nothing to me. So much of my cognitive processes remained underdeveloped.

The scientists were very jovial, jocular with each other and even with me, but I understood little of their humor. They had a penchant for calling things by initials. Dr. Zerjeff they usually called Dr. E.Z. Some called me R.C. — Restoration Child. HTZ was for Hematostretz, DVA was Dermavitae. There was something inside of me identified as TITS the mention of which seemed to arouse special hilarity. Dr. Zerjieff, as a matter of fact, frequently chastised the group for what she deemed unseemly humor at my expense. Sometimes she attempted to explain to me the amusing aspect of some remark, but I really could not reach any understanding.

Understanding seemed like that to me, a reaching. I felt myself reach and reach but all that actually came under the control of my understanding was the shapes of things. Apparently the Vetrumfoculi which had been placed in my eye sockets were especially keen this way. I saw Dr. E.Z. as a massive form. She had a small head atop smallish shoulders and, as the eye traveled downward, she grew larger and larger. I made special note of this configuration. It was comforting to me that, in her long white robes, the doctor resembled an upended cone. I had not yet succeeded in differentiating the other specialists and technicians. They were perceived by me as a group of cylindrical shapes. A few were like rectangular solids of varying length or width. Their heads, no matter how brilliant they were said to be, were mere ovules.

Many times I heard Dr. E.Z. declare that the aglommeration that was me had required the combined genius of dozens of renowned intellects. Doctors of medicine, chemistry, psychology, even engineers and physical architects had had their part in this enterprise. According to Dr. E.Z. even historians and poets had been brought into the cooperative venture. All were individuals of world renown, as was I.

And so I was. Dr. E.Z. assured me that I once was a pioneering mathematician, responsible for theories that were about to revolutionize established principles of mathematical thought. That is, I had been. She was determined to bring back to the world the author of such valuable contributions. Toward this end she worked on restoring my mental faculties. She talked to me incessantly. She talked to me about my past, the details of both my professional and personal past.

"There are still traces of your original components. Traces of your personal ingredients," she said. "As we have restored viable life to your remains so may we restore sentience, individuality, personhood, participation in life. Do you understand?"

I did not.

"Personality. Feeling."

Nothing stirred in me.

"You are quite presentable. We made sure to give you a broad brow, reasonably human features. You could attract someone, maybe even someday make love," she said.

I was utterly blank. There were in my mind obtuse shapes that floated, but not a scintilla of understanding came with them.

"That means you could look forward to having sex again," she said rather sharply.

I understood something but I could not say what. It was certainly not anything like what seemed to be stirring the doctor to her patient efforts. Rather it was a cavernous void in which there was an echoing solitude.

When she talked to me, nudging me about the person she said I had been, she always said, "Do you remember?" over and over again.

Well, yes. I did remember things, I think. I remembered hollow shapes. They had meaning but I could not quite discern it. I could not sort out the meaning of many concepts. It seemed to me that all things had a meaning within a meaning within a meaning. I could remember words but I could not get to the core of them. I remembered them but, in the very moment of remembering them, they were not there. They escaped. They were empty shapes like the people that surrounded me.

The Restoration was a portentous venture. Millions had gone into the research that led into the successful articulation of the Restoration Child. Dr. E.Z. had every confidence that I would justify the expense of money and time.

But I died in the accident.

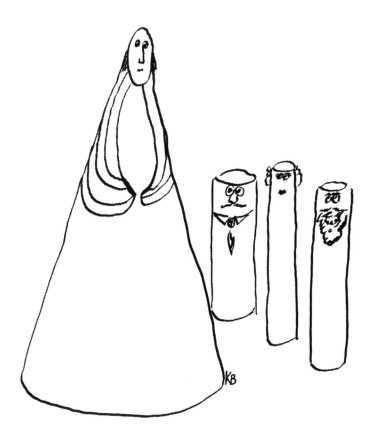

WHEN THE SCREEN WAS REALLY SILVER

IN LATE NIGHT ALBERT and Joany watch the old movies. They love the oldies. There's nothing nowadays to match those deep black shadows and the gleam of satiny white. Just the contrasts make a narrative telling a big part of the tale. The perfect make-up, the stylish clothes, smooth movement, studied camera angles, perfect faces, stories that satisfy. What do they care if the ending is predictable, the world made into an unreal illusion? Illusion is what they come for. They love the predictability.

It's the safe old world that the two can still remember. Boys met girls and that led to love and that led to marriage and, if the film was long enough, that led to babies. Any heart aches conveniently resolved, all happy in the end.

They especially like to identify old actors. Albert and Joany share a real joy in recognizing old faces. They are welcome old acquaintances dropping in from a friendlier world.

"Who is that guy, Honey? He was in a million films."

"I know! He always played gangsters or Indians or Egyptians but he was really Italian. Eduardo… Eduardo something…"

"Cianelli!" Albert exclaims and they both sink back into the sofa, pleased and happy.

"Alby, look who's tangling with Bette Davis. Miriam Hopkins!"

"Yeah," he replies. "I hope she slugs her, pops her a good one." But Bette is going to win. All the conventions of old films – everything, the facial expressions, the postures, the camera's approach – make it clear that Bette is the good girl and Miriam is the heavy. Albert just doesn't like Davis. "A lousy actress. She's all snotty and stylized," he always says. "No American talks like that."

"It doesn't matter," Joany says. She doesn't agree.

"Right. Both dead now, anyhow." He sighs and takes his pipe.

A pretty girl wanders across the screen. According to the old canon of proper style, she's wearing hat to match bag and gloves to match shoes. Her tailored suit is something from the pages of Vogue.

"One of those sisters," Albert says.

"The Lanes. Priscilla Lane. Remember this film, Alby? She's supposed to be an unemployed, impoverished shop girl. Check the million dollar clothes she's wearing." He smiles. They love these contrasts. Isn't this magical inconsistency what films are for? "She was so pretty, wasn't she?"

"Yeah," he agrees, "but probably dead."

Albert puffs on an empty pipe. He gave up tobacco years ago.

Another film comes on. They know this one. They see Hepburn. "Katie. She looks so wonderfully young, Alby."

"How can you stand her?" he says. "She's just as stylized and snotty and even stiffer than Davis ever was."

"I like them both," Joany replies.

"But not George Brent?"

"He's sleazy."

"You say that about every actor with a mustache."

"They taught us to hate mustaches in the old serials. Remember Duncan Renaldo?"

Albert hisses just as he used to in the old days.

Now they go into another film, a story, a little world of dreams, different pretty young girls fill the screen. These faces are very familiar though still so young, almost children. Only little embryos of what they were to become. "Oh, Lucille Ball," Joany announces, "but pre-Lucy, Lucille Ball as a baby!"

"So young," Albert agrees, "before she got comical. Just a pretty little starlet. Wouldn't you like to go back in time and tell her how famous she was going to become?"

"Famous and rich," Joany agrees.

"Famous. And rich. And dead."

"Alby, look. Here's that little actress. The sad one. The camera has her set up for a tragedy. You know she will end badly from the first minute she comes on screen. What was her name? Andrea… Andrea something…"

"Leeds," he says. Albert is proud that he still has a memory. Sometimes.

"You know they're going to sacrifice her. Bump her off to make the story work." Joany remarks. They're almost like gods, Albert and Joany. Everything is so predictable. It would be even if they had not seen this film about a hundred times.

"This gal's a stinker," Albert says. Gail Patrick just came on. "She always played bitches. The minute you spotted her you knew she was going to do something dastardly. And to top it all off she's with Adolphe Menjou."

Joany hisses this time.

Albert chuckles. "Well, he does have a mustache," he says. Albert thinks Joany's mustache aversion is funny because he just grew one. Now Eve Arden's on. "Always a bridesmaid, never a bride," Albert remarks.

Then next there comes a film they haven't seen before, an ancient musical. A row of girls are dancing. So lovely. It's tap. So delightfully crisp. The sound of their feet tapping is like a salvo of pop pistols, very synchronized. There must be twenty-five young women in that line up. They are perfect. All of the same size and shape. Coordinated. Syncopated. They're dressed in Scottish costumes, kilts with sporrans, high socks, plaid scarves, tam o'shanters though the choreography is pure Hollywood, has nothing to do with the Highland Fling. These are inconsistencies that Albert and Jody love. It's something they watch for affectionately.

The camera glides across the twenty-five pretty faces, each baring a glorious smile. Brilliant smiles. Gorgeous teeth. Flashing eyes. There is not a familiar face among them. "None of them made it," Albert comments, "Betcha every one of those gals was expecting to be discovered,"

"Sad," Joany says by way of agreement. She can see how hard they're trying. They are in thrall to the popular mythology as we, in our innocence, all used to be. The little hoofer in the chorus would be discovered. By some fortuitous accident – like the star's broken foot, or broken heart, or temper tantrum – the lead would not go on. The desperate director tearing his hair until someone called out, "Go get that little girl with the big smile! She knows the part!" Who would say that? Maybe the leading man. Then the audience knew at once that in the picture he would end up totally in love with her. By all progressions of fictional development that was inevitable. He would love the little hoofer, now a star, and it would be Sally Whoever. Our gal Sally! How satisfying!

Only it never happened. Not a one of those faces in the line ever became famous. Albert and Joany knew. They were film addicts from way back.

"Well, at least they got their little moment on film," Albert says.

"Something to tell their grandchildren," comments Jody.

"Maybe great-grandchildren," he says. "How old do you figure those babes would be now?"

"Mmmm. Older than we are. If alive."

And they are silent for a while. Sad. Thinking of all those dreams never realized, of all those fresh young faces eroding, smiles hardened into dentures, eyes dimming. Sad, but why should it be so sad? They are just the same, Albert and Joany, diminishing but not sad. He smokes his fake pipe. They look at each other. He smiles his funny smile. She likes his mustache. It makes him look distinguished.

"Not dead," he says to her, and he takes her hand.

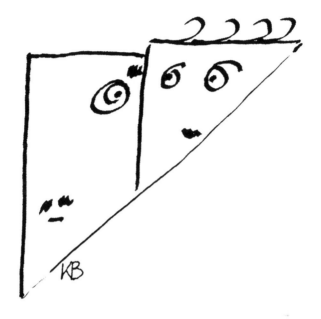

JUST JUNK

THE HORROR SHOP IS really going good now. The Bay Ridge store got so busy I had to open a branch in Bensonhurst and that one really took fire too: it's going better than the first actually. Mail orders are taking off on me. I've applied for patents on a couple of new gadgets and I can tell you right now they are going to make it big. It won't be giving too much away if I tell you they involve viscous liquids and offensive smells. Real yukkers. Sure things. The kids'll love them. What? The kids? Everybody! I may go worldwide. Even the Brits have started doing Halloween now. And that's why I'm at Heathrow this day, looking at a display in a bookshop when on the cover of a dark bound book I see this authoress. Yeah. Turbaned. Ha! Austere. Hollow-eyed. Evil. And am I cracking up! The turban. The name! *Diocletia Mondragone* is what it says on there but it's really Alma, Alma Beidecker, my childhood crony. Jeez. Grade Seven. William McKinley JHS on Fort Hamilton Parkway of Brooklyn, New York! A long time ago, she's come a long way from pigtails and braced teeth, but I'd know that Alma anywhere.

She looks like the Delphic Oracle or something. Deep. If pictures could talk this one would have a voice like an echo in a cavern. Doom. Doom. Doom. Like that. Or like an echo in a garbage can. Because she's written another garbage book. Yeah. Two of them have already been made into movies. *Bloodflower* is what she's called this one and she's filled it with stories of horror and disgust like we used to tell on the corner of Ovington Avenue in the days when we weren't above enumerating the ingredients of the scab sandwiches we'd like to feed the boys. If only I could look into her living face right now I know she'd crack. We'd be laughing our heads off again, just like we used to in our baby days.

I know all these ideas started fermenting in her devious head that one chilly day a lot of years ago. We were together that day when this devil guy popped up at the 16B bus stop. He belched a little fire at us. A pot-bellied little guy he was. Kind of ruddy. Alma must have turned away to giggle because she didn't see that next he hitched up his little tail and a puff of smoke shot out of his backside which really flipped me out. She kept laughing her head off anyway because she saw me laughing. Whaddaya want? At thirteen it's the law. You're <u>supposed</u> to giggle at everything. Like in school. It made the teachers crazy which made us do it more. Our favorite thing to do was identify who farted. Like it was one of the most important things in life. And we'd say things like, "Quit picking your nose! Why can't you wait 'til lunch?" and die laughing. Or you could get in a fight with some girl and, when she got close, heave off real disgusted, hold your nose, yell something like, "Don't you <u>ever</u> wash your hair?" which would kill the fight because all the kids would be laughing at her, actually rolling around the ground. We'd say things like, "Hey! That Diana Cimaduomo is so full of zits even Mr. Zacker rejected her!" Scream. Slap your thighs. Mr. Zacker was the janitor. He smelled like the jakes. Kids loved to make up funny stories that he was a child molester.

Anyhow the little devil guy got on the bus with us. Very friendly, grinning like he knew a dirty secret, so bad we had to like him. He started up with us when we went by the deaf school. The kids there were a kick. They were so obvious. They couldn't pass whispers, and too young to be subtle. All of them could see what everybody else was talking about. You could tell in a minute who was friends, who was sick with love, who was ready to murder who. The devil nudged us. He was jerking his head toward two boys. "Fairyland. Fairyland. Look at those two," he said. "Queer as three dollar bills." They were making these signs that would knock you out. One of them looked as if he was conducting an orchestra. The other would interrupt. He'd about sock the first one, and, then, it was like he had a big sack of words by his side and he would reach his hand into it, pick out a real lollapalooza word, dust it off on his leg, and shove it in the other kid's face.

"Did you ever see anyone lisp in sign language before?" the devil said. We almost fell into the aisle at that. "*The Silent Swish*," Alma announced. She was forever rhyming things or making up titles. We laughed till it hurt. The devil's eyes got red with tears, or acid, whatever the hell devils have.

A woman was sitting a few seats in front of us. Her baby would pop up over her shoulder, sort of lean over to stare at us. The woman didn't know it but the baby was drooling buckets all over her velvet jacket. The kid had slanty eyes, sort of a blank look, like an elf or a deficient. "I'll get that kid someday," the devil said. "It's got the same look as this guy I know. Of course, he's mine already. He keeps this carnivorous plant. *Crapulina skifosa* he calls it. I think he bred it himself. Probably out of an insect eater but he got it to grow really big. He tried to feed it a mouse once. He held the mouse by the tail and the plant's lobules grabbed the head. Then spat it out. Like it coughed. The mouse plopped out. The lobes were all covered with gray fluff and the mouse's head had no eyes anymore. Just a pink veined blob at the end of the body. It smelled just like the plant by then, too, like ripe cheese."

"*Gross of mouse,*" intoned Alma and I yelled, "Yukk!" in protest, but both of us were laughing like hyenas.

The bus stopped for a light. He got all excited. "Quick. Look over there!" he said. A man was standing on the corner, really standing because in full sight of God and everybody he was fingering his stiff wiener a mile a minute. The whole while his face was a marvel of dignity and importance. In fact he looked a little bit like Mr. Scudderbeake who was the principal of our school, especially when Scudderbeake would stand in front of a whole assembly and wait loftily for the kids to get silent. Pompous as the king of the world. Alma and I really loved this. Now we could always guess what Scudderbeake might be doing behind the lectern. This devil really had our attention now. He was pointing things out. He was making us see what he saw. "You wanna see some more?" he said.

"Yeah."

"It costs."

"Yeah. Right." I was holding my sides because Alma kept crossing her eyes at me.

"No money. Just junk," he said, sniggering like a maniac, just as hard as we were. "Okay? Hey!" he yelled. "Look at the way that guy drives his cart." A big handsome man was standing on top of a dray cart with his legs spread out, a whip in his hand, knowing he could make the poor nag do whatever he wanted. "That's the way he does with his women at night," the devil said. We laughed, but it was a little uneasy. I'd never seen a dray wagon on 86th Street before. We weren't actually in Brooklyn anymore. At least, I didn't think so. A killing sun was coming up. In spite of devastating heat we went through more than one puddle and the puddles were getting so dark they looked like pools of blood. The sun etched out shadows of things sharply. Horns. Offal of slaughtered animals. Rams, maybe. Huge birds were circling down to pick it over. "That's for the sacrifice," the devil explained. We just looked at each other and smiled kind of stupidly. We weren't sure if we should laugh or not.

Pammy Montjou was walking toward the bus right through one of the red puddles. She didn't seem to notice it even though it was splashing stuff right up her high white socks. She was our age but very voluptuous and she was walking with her belly thrust forward, a little duck-toed. "You can already see her body's gotta dictate the kind of woman she's gonna be," the devil said importantly. "There's already something in the oven, too." We were a little dense. It was a new expression to us. "PG," he explained. In a deliberately droll voice he added. "Her papa put it to her." We giggled at that. Just then the bus zoomed off. Pammy slipped in the red puddle. Sat down like a sack. The look on her face was so funny we screamed. Alma said, *Plop in the glop*, sort of like a book title, so we doubled over. "I think I'm gonna pee my pants," she gasped, and that was guaranteed to make us scream louder.

Out by the lots he pointed out a field of thistle-like flowers by the side of the road. They stuck out stiff heads, flaming red. "Those pinch," the devil said, "but they make the best dried arrangements. Odoriferous. Gelatinous. Mucilaginous," he intoned as if making a kind of churchy litany. "They bloom at the end of tendrils which originate in pleated wastes."

"*Gloomblooms*! I want some!" Alma cried. "I do flower arrangements."

"Well, I know that," the little devil said smugly. In that very moment I could kind of smell him. I was surprised that people who smell very ripe can still speak and smile with such sweet civility, like I was always surprised that boys who looked like warty carbuncles would always want to get close to you, press their knobby bodies at you instead of hiding them in shame the way they should.

He pointed out the house on Endicott Drive where the old woman was murdered by the guy who drove the bakery truck. "He made her eat his doodles," the devil said. We kind of smiled. It was such a funny way of saying it. But it wasn't really so easy to laugh even though we sure used to laugh at that old woman when she was alive. She was kind of doddery and friendly but really ugly, all bumps and creases. Some people said she had been a great beauty once. But people always say that about old people. She had great big choppers, white as toilet porcelain, and she had no control over them. Sometimes they bit off her words before she was finished saying them. You could die laughing. The killer did all kinds of violent stuff to her. They say he impaled her. She was still alive through that. The funny part is that everyone knew the delivery guy. Everybody did. He seemed a nice guy. Kind of quiet. Alma and I almost had a crush on him because he had this great crest of fiery red hair. But the papers said that to the end he remained furious, unrepentant. "She let me in," he'd said. "So she had it coming."

I stared at the house. "He asked to go in to use the bathroom," I said. "The guy just must have gone crazy."

"No," the devil said in a most reasonable voice. "He told her he had hermatochezia. She didn't know what that was. She had it coming. He was right, your red-combed rooster."

And for some reason that just convulsed us, maybe because he seemed to know about our crush on that killer-tussock. We laughed uncontrollably.

"He's mine, too," the devil said. "I got a lot. Maybe you girls don't believe I know you. Your mother is Nadine," he said to Alma. "Right?"

"*Nadine the Nicotine Queen.* Yeah."

"She smokes so many cigarettes she can't talk anymore, right? She growls." It was right but before I could start to laugh he turned to me. "Your mama's Juanita." I about exploded out at that. Ma would die. She hated her name. She made everybody call her Trixie. "Part of her is always in the commode," he added thoughtfully. Yeah! Right! I'd just argued with old Trixie because she always blotted her lipstick on the toilet paper. You'd go in and you'd find a pair of lips floating around in the bowl.

Alma held a laugh in her mouth till her cheeks bulged out. Then she blew it all out. She just about doubled to the floor.

"You gals are perfect and you're mine now," the devil said contentedly.

"Whaddaya mean?"

"How many people are on this bus?"

We made a quick count. "*I've seen thirteen*," Alma said in her poetic way.

"Right," said the little man. "And, as you know, if there are thirteen at the table, one of them will always be Judas Iscariot, but if there are thirteen on the bus, one of them is bound to be a little devil."

You probably don't even believe in the devil, so this won't make a whole lot of sense to you, but we cracked, Alma and I. We loved it. "Wait a minute!" I yelled. "We haven't made any deal."

"Yes, we have," said the devil. "A few pages ago. It went by without you noticing. You gotta be quick. Everything really important happens in the blinking of an eye."

"Hold it! Hold it! We're supposed to get something. What do <u>we</u> get out of this?"

"Oh, I'm gonna give you a great gift," he said with a flourish. "A gift that will enhance your appreciation and your skills for the particular world in which you now live. I'm gonna give you, in perpetuity, the perceptions, the reactions, the emotions and the hearts of adolescents."

And there you are.

I'm making a pile out of it. And look at Alma. Everybody reads her stuff. The films they make of them feature special effects that make strong men barf. I, mean, yeah! Wonderful! I think of that whenever I hear some old fart say, "What ever happened to good taste? What ever happened to refinement and discretion in this world?"

Oh, and yeah, we went back for those thistle flowers that day. But we couldn't pick them. Near where the bums hung out they were growing right out of a sewer ditch, stinking of human excrement.

"I guess they must be *poo-toonias*," Alma said. We laughed about an hour at that.

THE HORNS OF PATSY NOFRIO

Pasquale Nofrio, called Patsy, was the Ice and Coal man who came to our back door both summer and winter in the old days. In winter he sent avalanches of coal down chutes into our cellar. In summer he lugged in huge chunks of ice to replenish the drippings in our old icebox. Patsy loved our mother. Not in any scandalous sense. Patsy simply thought our little mother was the nicest, most civilized person of his acquaintance which was, of course, quite true. She always invited him in for *caffe latte* just as if he were a gentleman in a white shirt. But, best of all, the lady spoke Sicilian. She understood him. He could talk with her and Patsy sorely needed the ear of some kind human because his heart was heavy. At his house, a home cursed with treacherous women and girls, he could talk to no one.

It was about his third daughter, Immacolata by name if not by habits. Immy Nofrio was in high school at the time. I went to P.S. 125 and used to see her across the field between the two schools. A short girl, very round, she was always hanging around with Jimmy Belcavallo. Her body was rotund like Patsy's and she was also blessed with his sweet face and normally benign expression. Not so benign was Patsy now, however, as he sat in our kitchen and told our mother his tragic tale.

Patsy loved Jimmy Belcavallo the same way he loved his Immy. The kids had been together since First Communion. Everyone knew they would marry some day. Nobody was surprised when they decided to drop out of school to do it. And to no particular opposition either, for in those days and in that family no one, neither Patsy nor his patient wife, Gemma, saw any real advantage to schooling. Besides Jimmy said he had a job waiting for him, which would have been pretty good news except that it happened to be so far off—in Chicago—which made both Gemma and Immy cry. Both of them had never envisioned anything other than a good Italo-American life in the same suburb of Brooklyn, maybe Bensonhurst, or Bay Ridge, or Dyker Heights, intervisiting from house to house at need or whim. Jimmy looked sad about moving, too, and though Patsy could already feel the absence of his daughter as an empty space gathering up future hurt in his heart, he was realistic. He amassed all he could of his ice and coal savings, as much as he could borrow, to throw a wedding, the fanciest wedding ever heard of. Everyone went. It was catered by the best *pasticceria* on Mulberry Street. Wine and whiskey flowed. Everything the best. There were even matchbooks, all white with golden letters spelling, intertwined, "Jimmy & Immy," in a script that everyone admired, especially my sister Loretta, who took home a pocketful. But that same night, their wedding night, so very sadly, Jimmy and Immaculata had to take the train to Chicago.

And then? Nothing.

A week. Nothing.

Another week. A postcard saying very little. And more nothing.

Gemma was going crazy. Nobody had a phone so, with great effort, she wrote long letters in a language she made up herself. Nobody answered.

It got murderously cold. The sun faded to a pale slice like a juiceless round of lemon in the hard sky. Pavements were ready to crack and splinter into shards of ice.

People ordered lots of coal. Patsy was working extra hours but as the joyous season approached there was no joy for him. Each night Gemma looked at him with haunted eyes. He could see his sweet woman wasting. "Pasquale, whaddaya think? Maybe somethin' happen to the kids? Somethin' bad?"

"Maybe just lazy," he'd say gruffly, but he didn't really believe that. Something was funny. When finally she could stand it no longer she announced she was going. Herself, Gemma Nofrio, going to go to Chicago!

Patsy was scared for her, but he told our mother he took her to the bus. She got to Chicago late that freezing night. Took a taxi, an incredible extravagance. Everything a great effort for poor Gemma in that alien city. She'd never been out of Brooklyn since her own Mama and Papa had brought her there, a small and scared Sicilian six-year-old so many years before. This was a giant matter for her; its importance gave her unexpected strength. She went to the address Jimmy and Immaculata had once scrawled on that single postcard.

It was a seedy walk-up in a seedier building. "*C'era 'na puzza!*" Gemma later remembered. *A stink.* The smell of alien cooking. She rang and rang. She could hear the bell squealing inside. With the special acuity of a mother's ears she also heard emptiness. Not a soul was in there. *N'ca? A mezzanotte? At midnight?* She rang so long and so hard that, finally, the neighbors came to the facing door to give her the dreadful news, news that seemed to stop her heart. *L'ospedale! Dio c'e ne scampi e liberi! Lord protect us. The hospital! Spare us, oh Lord!*

Santa Rosalia must have helped, she said later. Some divine intervention. Because the same taxi driver was still downstairs, as if waiting for her. Even Chicago had its good Italian boys and this one had taken a special interest in Gemma, so plain and unkempt and distraught. He stayed with her the rest of that dramatic night, as if he were a son of her very own family. He took her to the terrible hospital.

Like a soul in purgatory, Jimmy was there. When he saw Gemma he began to cry. Big whooping sobs that Gemma would never forget. "Mama!" he cried, hugging her so tight she could hardly breathe. "Oh, Mama! Help us!" he pleaded. He was eighteen years old but looked ancient and like a little boy at the same time. An old man who couldn't take any more and a lost boy—because Immaculata was in the other room bringing forth their baby. A baby! And only three months married! *Santa Maria! 'Na disgrazia! A disgrace!*

There would be Patsy, telling this to our mother. Always, at this point, he would make gestures as if tearing at his own cheeks. He'd roll his eyes and look at Mama. *"A mea, Signora! A mea! M'fatto i corni!"* She'd put the horns on him. And she had. Immy'd put the horns on him, disgraced him good, disgraced Patsy and his whole line by marching down that aisle decked out in white as nice as you please but with a belly on her that her stout little body had somehow managed to conceal. Fixing it so later everybody could have a good laugh on Patsy Nofrio. No wonder they were so nervous. No wonder such a hurry to go to Chicago!

"So what happened, Signor Nofrio?" our mother would say.

"What happened, Signora? They come back. Back to Brooklyn. Gemma, she help them. They got no money. Full of debts. What job? He had no job, that *minchione, schiagurato, ai'male!* It was just a big story to put horns on me. On me, that loved him so much! *L'ai'male!* Animal, he called Jimmy Belcavallo, and then bit his fingers to show his rage.

"She's here now, your daughter?"

"*Idda?* Not my daughter no more. I tell Gemma—she goes to those *porchi di maiale, those swine!* I kill her with these hands!"

"Signor Nofrio!" It was our mother's cue to plead mercy. She obliged. "*Sanguzzo di vossia sunnu! They're your very own blood!*"

But Patsy would shake his head, his fists clenched, his eyes wild.

We knew Gemma Nofrio was cheating. Jimmy had gotten a job on the docks in Red Hook. They were scrimping, just getting along. The shame-faced couple had taken a one-room apartment only a block from the Nofrio house. When Gemma knew Patsy was making deliveries in another part of the town she would scurry over there with jars of good sauce and homemade sausages, the skinny kind with cheese and parsley and the seeds of *finocchio* minced right in with the meat, the kind Immy absolutely loved to gorge on. What else could Gemma do? There was in that house a baby of her very own blood. A beautiful boy. Fat and handsome. Already clever enough to smile at his *nonna*. So she lied to Patsy. Everyone in the neighborhood knew it.

Patsy remained adamant. Days passed. Oh, let it be set out here in brittle words, Patsy Nofrio was a hard hard man.

But there had to come a day. One icy morning he came out of a driveway from one of his deliveries and there was Immaculata pushing the carriage. Before his face could set in hate, before he could bite his fingers in the rage of his disgrace, his eyes beheld the bundle in the carriage.

It was like some mirror in which time had collapsed. There was a little Patsy in there! Himself! Small! "Sant' Antonio!" he yelled over and over, loud enough for people to come to their windows to see what the commotion could be, and Patsy began to cry. Immy was in his arms, as if she had materialized there, as if she had never been anywhere else, wetting his ears with her tears. Sobbing, they hugged each other hard enough to make up for the pain all of them had suffered in that cruel time.

Saint Anthony had found for Patsy Nofrio something precious he thought lost forever.

And then Patsy was in our kitchen again, accepting mother's interest and her *caffè latte*. "*Signora, ora ho 'na devozione—a devotion to discharge,*" he declared. It was important. A vow that went with a change of heart imposed upon him by a saint. He was collecting money. He was going to give it to Saint Anthony through the church down in Little Italy. They would buy the bread to feed the poor. *U panuzzu.* Of course, our mother would help. She was enchanted.

"What did they name the baby, Mr. Nofrio?" asked Loretta, who at that time of her life was interested in the names of babies. She had at least twenty three of her future babies named in her school notebook. Their last names fluctuated with the name of whatever pimply boy had caught her notice at the time. Patsy gave a sheepish grin. "Like me," he said in his brusque way. "Only in French. Noel."

"Noel means Christmas in French," said smartie Loretta. "Pasquale doesn't mean Christmas."

"No," he agreed. "Whaddaya call? Easter! I was born Easter time. *Pasqua.* The baby was born Christmas time. *Noel.*"

It was still Christmas season too, I remember. The *Befana* had come with Epiphany presents that very morning. And, even better, the bitterest cold had broken and the new day had dawned with a blessed cover of white snow.

THE JOE SHOW

ONE NIGHT I DREAMT that my head was a mailbox. My left ear was adjustable, contrived to slide up to indicate the presence of outgoing mail. In order to receive mail the front of my face folded down like a drawbridge. Gus, the regular mailman, was a sweetie. He handled me with care. The substitute mail guy, though, was another story altogether. He had no respect for my hinges, crammed the mail in, and slammed me shut again. I felt thoroughly slapped. I was indignant but there wasn't a damn thing I could do about it. I was rooted to the ground as if someone had shoved a ramrod up my ass. Though I could not see downward, I was pretty sure my nether regions had solidified in some nefarious way. I felt I had no arms to punch with and no legs to kick with. I had nothing left alive but flapping mouth and mailbox head.

As if that weren't bad enough, the mail started coming in. Catalogs came. They were fat and chunky. Pulp paper. Talk about choking! Then came the offers for insurance, for new mortgage arrangements, for credit cards that promised cash rewards, two-for-one dinners, prizes, magazine subscriptions and free airline tickets. Next the charities came on board for their share. Animal Rights sent pictures of molested lions. Apparently there was no limit to the outrages visited upon dogs, cats, chickens, horses and aardvarks. Every disease in the annals of medicine felt free to send me photos or descriptions of their most scrofulous conditions. Right into my passive mouth went the pox, the plague, and pustules of galloping leprosy.

Then I was regaled with unsolicited little presents calculated to induce guilt. Avalanches of address labels arrived. Everyone sent those. Emblems and bumper stickers. Bookmarks. Calendars for 2011 began to appear. I estimated that, starting at this early date, by the New Year I would have a collection of at least a hundred calendars. The Native American tribes sent minute little dream catchers and tiny cardboard effigies of Kokopeli playing his flute. Missions of holy women sent crucifixes woven of straw. The blind wanted me to have their cards that were embossed with the Braille alphabet. The Alzheimer's Research people sent me pads of reminder notes.

Wouldn't you think that in this inundation of postal trash some personal epistles might appear? No such luck. The only thing resembling real mail was a scattering of postcards from Joe. They came from faraway places like Surinaam, Rekjavik, Maprao and they all bore the kind of messages that say nothing, "HELLO!" or "GREETINGS!" except for one card that bore only cryptic letters, "HANL."

When I told about it at the breakfast table Covina started laughing so hard she spilled her coffee into the eggs. You know Covina. Such a slobby pig. Her dirty blonde hair was up in curlers that were so big they looked loaves of bread. She began hooting like an owl.

"It's not funny!" I protested.

"Oh, yes it is. So so funny," she said. She's always ready to put me down.

"It was a nightmare," I insisted.

"Well, you say so, but you've got to admit the picture of Gus shoving junk mail down your gullet is pretty funny."

Of course, that was true. The details were ludicrous – mailbox head, earflap flag, rebar spine – but you know how dreams can have an aura. Some dreams, though the details are mundane and even nonsensical, bear an ominous quality that permeates everything, as if music from a scary movie played in the background. Sometimes, that music lingers in your brain long after awakening.

"Let me tell you this," Covina said in her snottiest big sister tone. "As far as Joe is concerned you can whistle Dixie, kiddo. Joe is good and gone for you whether he went to Timbuctu or around the corner to Magruder Street."

Oh, mean. So mean. Covina is so mean. You know what she's like. She's such a bitch. Has to be at the center of everything. Probably wishing she'd been the one to have the mailbox-head dream. She's so jealous of my petite size when she comes out big as a mail truck. And she wasn't done mocking yet either. She started speculating. "What do you think that HANL could be?"

I had stopped answering. I was good and sore. I knew she was going to make as much out of it as she could. "Hanl!" she exclaimed in mock delight. "Hanl! Hanl! That stands for a girl's name. I bet that's it. Two'll get you three he had a thing going with that Hanna Lee slut that works at the video shop. If you'll pardon the expression, Joe was just a big time fuckmeister."

Laughing. Ha. Ha. Braying like a donkey.

Just then I accidentally spilled my orange juice all over Covina's fat lap. "You asshole!" she yelled.

"Jackass!" I replied.

She was at me in a flash and I was ready to reply with words or punches or fingernails or whatever she threw me, but our brother, Larry, intervened. He held me by the nape of the neck, the way he does. I think he uses holds on us that he learned when he was on the high school wrestling team. That's about all he did learn in high school, too. "Who do you think wrote those cards you saw in your dream?" he said.

"Joe!" I told him.

"No. Not Joe. Think about it."

I was still under the influence of the eerie dream mood later that same day when I met Gladys Looper, my best friend, in the SuperX. She walked toward me kind of hoity-toity, the way she walks. Her hair was bright orange. She wanted everyone to see her new dye job. "What's the matter with you?" she said. "You look like a boiled sea slug." So I told her all about the dream and the cryptic cards and HANL and how mean Covina was and everything.

"You know Joe?" I said.

"Joe LoPinto?" Of course she knew him. All the girls know Joe. "Where is he anyhow?"

"Disappeared," I told her.

"I believe he's trying to communicate where he is with those cards"

"Then he's everywhere, in South America, Russia, Iceland, Africa, the south seas, and a bunch of countries that don't even exist anymore. But I don't really care where he is. It's the HANL that drives me nuts."

"HANL?"

"Yeah. The word on the card. Covina thinks he had a thing with Hanna Lee, that slutty girl in the video shop."

"Joe had a thing with almost everybody so what does Covina know? That little ho in the video shop is not called Hanna Lee, anyhow. Her name is Francine. Your sister knows from nothing. She's such an idiot. She just has to wag her big butt into everything."

Gladys has her issues with Covina too.

You know I hardly ever dream but the very next night I dreamt my entire head was in the aquarium. I don't mean my head <u>was</u> the actual tank but just <u>in</u> it, rooted by the neck in filthy gravel. There were fish in there, too, some nervous little guppies and a pair of pink gouramis that kept trying to kiss me with their nasty fish lips. My hair was swirling around with the tides and the guppies kept darting in and out of it as if it were a brake of water reeds. Sporadically a stream of tiny bubbles issued from my nose and ascended to the surface. With all this going on my ability to see was practically zilch and, of course, I couldn't hear a thing. The fish tank was placed directly in front of the television set and now I glimpsed something that made me strain against the low visibility. Grainy and vague on the old Philco there had momentarily appeared the face of Joe LoPinto!

It was The Joe Show! I tried to focus through the confusion of swirling hair, restless guppies, amorous gouramis, and columns of trapped air escaping from my own nose.

Letters were bobbing around. I spotted a couple of B's. I couldn't tell if they were merely junk in the aquarium water or something flashing across the TV screen. I was really straining to get Joe's face together. He had a handsome face but that didn't stop him from being a bastard. Then, just as I separated out all the flotsam and jetsam a bunch of cars appeared. A god-damned commercial! Everything got confused again. There was a big flush of bubbles from somewhere. The lousy gouramis were kissing away at my nose. Joe reappeared indistinctly. His lips moved. I couldn't hear him but I can tell you right now anything Joe said would have to be lies. Of course, all I actually could hear was the gushes and gurgles and the little fish kisses that made a minute sucking sound. It was a dirty dream. Don't think I was not cognizant of the fact that at that very moment those hyperactive little guppies were probably peeing all over my personal space.

Joe came back into sight. He was lipping something at me when, suddenly, his face transmogrified into a big pizza pie. Family size. Pepperoni with anchovies. The pizza was happy. It wore a huge grin. Joe peeked around a corner of the crust and words streamed out of his mouth as if printed on a ribbon.

This is what it said: HAVE A NICE LIFE.

SEX AND SORROW IN THE OLD COUNTRY

A True Story

IN THE HOLIDAYS OUR mother and her cousin Eufemia whispered of our *padrino*, who was Papa's dear old friend, Alfredo D'Amico. They did not giggle at this tale. It was a sad one.

He was an old man but he had befriended Papa when he first came to the New World and Papa dearly loved him. Mama invited him to dinner almost every Sunday. Our parents would fill him with good food. I think he needed it. Eventually he'd lean back, undoing the top button of his trousers to accommodate the magnificent meal, groaning his contentment. That was something that always visibly pleased our little mother. She didn't even mind the ensuing cigar.

He always brought the Sunday funnies and a bar of Suchard chocolate for each of us children. He was a man who radiated kindness and a gentleness of heart that all of us felt, even though there was a note of sorrow behind it. He often smiled, but seldom laughed. And he had the biggest nose we ever saw. *"Come 'na tabaccaia,"* our mother used to say. "Like a tobacco pouch."

Hard as it was for me to believe, Mama and Eufemia were saying that he was once a young and dapper man. He lived, then, in a village in Campagnia. In the normal course of events he became betrothed to one Angelina Benincasa, a local virgin renowned for her beauty and piety. Angelina seemed well pleased with the arrangement and young Alfredo was in heaven over it. He adored her. Her softness, her innocence, the trust in the look she bestowed on him, made his heart open each time he even thought of her.

There was the usual long engagement while Alfredo swinked to put together the cottage, the silver, the plate, the money for the all-important nuptial bed. Angelina's people, among the wealthiest of the village, were providing linens, everything made of cloth, everything soft to go into matrimony with the soft maiden.

Alfredo visited several times a week but, as was only right and proper, he saw Angelina only in the bosom of a batch of Benincasas. There were Benincasas everywhere with their brown eyes looking. The young couple never even held hands.

At last came the wedding. Wine and songs and smirks passed around along with that cruel banter that frequently masquerades as affection. They all knew that the young bride, as a girl of good and proper family, was headed for a revelation for which no one had ever prepared her. And the youngest of the women were the quickest to smirk since they themselves had recently undergone the amazing transition from girl to woman, and some of them at abrupt and brutal hands. Pleasant young Alfredo was not expected to be brutal but, of course, enamored as he was, excited and totally inexperienced, probably inept.

Some were still awake when, at a very late hour, the door of the Alfredo's little cottage burst open and Angelina ran out into the night. Her golden hair streamed, her eyes were wild, she wore her rumpled nightclothes, and she was screaming in unmistakable hysteria, *"E una bestia! E una bestia!"* Her new groom had come upon her with behavior that her upbringing told her was bestial. A sin of the worst order.

Alfredo, heartsore and terribly frightened, stood in the window in a nightshirt as virginally white as Angelina's while the village laughed.

Word had spread to the *taverna* and the men had already guffawed the night away. They had launched into wild and funny tales of their own initiations which became ever more vulgar, ever more boastful and exaggerated.

By morning all the wives knew it. They smiled with greater or lesser empathy, remembering. It was all over the village by morning that Angelina Benincasa would not submit. In the history of that village this was not the first instance of a green bride flushed from the bed by the insult of new conjugality. Time and nature always healed it, they thought. A woman must bow, bow to the inevitable. Bow to rude nature.

But Angelina was made of stronger stuff. She knew. It was wrong. There had been saints among her ancestors. She cleaved to the tradition of Agatha, of Ursula. In her case nature bowed, not she. Her education was too rigid and she had accepted it unequivocally. She could not open to Alfredo the treasure which he craved and to which, in the natural order of things, he had every right.

Even the Benincasas were appalled. They were an upright family, a family of means and respect. This was a matter of property to them. They felt that she had caused them to default on a contract. Her presence in their house shamed them. They sent at once for the village priest.

Don Domenico had been the source of much of the information that had influenced Angelina in the first place, but he was a realist too. He had in his own rectory, as everyone knew, a plump and complacent housekeeper who had the advantage of being barren. So he applied himself assiduously to the re-education of Angelina Benincasa. He gentled, he wheedled, he explained nature, he exhorted the heavenly host, advised her to better observe God's animals in the fields, he reasoned, he stormed, and, finally, he ended by shouting, disparaging, condemning her.

Angelina wept, blushed, trembled, but she would not budge. The soft little girl was obdurate, a little boulder. The act was not only sinful to her mind, but very very dirty in every way. She could not participate. If need be she would be like Ursula and seek her martyrdom.

And martyrdom she got. She was laughed at. Mocked. She was discounted as a viable woman. She dared not appear in the town. Not even at the window. Small children, who had no idea what the problem was, gathered outside to sing her name in ridicule. It made no difference to her resolve. She kept her head high knowing her course was a noble one.

And poor Alfredo. Enamored still, he almost took her side. He thought that what she said was probably true. He *was* a beast with animal cravings. Now he had no choice but to appear each day in the marketplace. He still had to earn his bread surrounded by the same men who so enjoyed deriding him. They called him a mouse for they could plainly see that rape had been the proper option and he could not bring himself to take it. Even his best friend told him that had he been any kind of man he would have thrust aside that maidenhead like so much trash. He began to believe himself something less than a man.

He was by trade a cart maker and a driver of the carts. At all his jobs and deliveries the cruel men openly laughed. It was a joke that never tired for them.

Frustrated, alone, with indescribable pain in his heart, Alfredo struggled along but the jostling never ceased. Sometimes it was virulent. It became so unbearable that Alfredo decided to abandon it all. He told only the priest, charging him to give the keys to the little cottage to Angelina. There she could reign in single solitude, attended by cats and saints, until she might grow to dodder and mumble and be seen, perhaps, as *una vecchia stregata*, a witch. As a reward for her chastity the village decreed her in league with the Evil One.

But Alfredo never knew her fate. He ran away.

He ran to the teeming city. In Naples he began again at the business he knew. As a lowly *carretiere* and having left most of his worldly goods with the virginal maiden, he had only enough to rent a simple room. Into it one night he took a woman who had cried piteously to him on the street of *Spaccanapoli*. She was a *malafemmina*, a bad woman, abused, ugly. She had a vicious scar on her face and it reflected what some man had thought of her. But she was as gentle with Alfredo as he was with her. With tender patience she taught him the pleasures he had never been allowed to indulge with his legitimate wife. This woman, Corinna, moved into Alfredo's modest room. She brought with her two bastards, children of fathers unknown. She did not disguise that fact that the fathers had only flickered through her life. And Alfredo loved the children anyway. He had an overwhelming ache to use his love. In need and gratitude, he loved and cared for them all in spite of the loose habits which Corinna and her brood never managed to overcome. One day, after a few years, when the boys were almost grown the three of them vanished. Alfredo had no word. He thought that perhaps, on the street of *Spaccanapoli,* Corinna had found someone much better than his poor self. Bereft, he begrudged her nothing.

"*Malavita,*" our mother said. Scum of Naples. The *Malavita* made Alfredo dare to emigrate though he was not such a young man anymore.

"He was a good soul," Eufemia said. "He deserved better of life. She and our mother looked at each other with glistening eyes.

"Some truths should never die though the people that lived them do, that's why we tell the tales," said Mama. To her cousin Eufemia she said that so much in life depended on pure Fortune. She agreed that *il padrino* had been a good soul. He had deserved better from the fates even though he had a nose like a tobacco pouch.

Except for the tobacco pouch most of this tale was mysterious to me as I sat in my little corner trying to make sense of the world.

SOMETHING SERIOUS

TWENTY YEARS LATER AND we're still co-habiting. They used to call it "living in sin," if that isn't the laugh riot of the century. Living in sin. It used to be called that anyhow. Without benefit of clergy, that's another laugh. By dint of longevity some would call it common-lawing, as if anyone cared. I don't. The only move I could make at this point in my life is to separate, and that would be too damned much trouble.

Look at the man. Any minute now he'll clear his throat. I know about it. Maybe he'll say, "I have this funny little knot in the side of my face settling in at the temple now. You think it could be something dangerous?"

Sure it could. Hopefully lethal. "Yes, dear." But he knows. He reads my aura. Insincerity.

Yesterday he looked up. Not really at me. He's always looking at something nobody else can see. He said, "The palms of my hands hurt."

"Are the soles of your feet okay?"

"Oh, I know," he muttered. "You think I'm nuts. You don't care. You don't take it seriously. But it could be a sign of something dangerous. Something serious."

Right now he is inside his own skin canvassing. His thought is like a restless tongue searching around the socket of a missing tooth. He's in contact with everything. Every bodily thing, that is. Maybe he is talking to his own spleen right now. Acting up? Of course. It would be. There's stuff about his prostate that's totally beyond my female comprehension, he says. Nowadays he constantly clears his throat. There's an obstruction there. "Something like a perpetual fog," he tells me.

Today he walked around the car four times. Yes, damn it. He checked the trunk. Up the driver's side, checking doors. Over to me to see if I had correctly secured the passenger side. Repeat. Four times around! Now it simmers in his mind. "I'm not sure if I locked the car."

"You locked it, Joey. You locked it. Besides, nobody wants it. Any real crook could get into it with a can opener."

"You don't care," he mutters. "They could walk off with the car, the house, everything. You wouldn't care." If it weren't for Joey they would have divested us of all but our skivvies long since. For the first really great laugh of this millennium, we'd be in our small clothes pulling squeaky supermarket carts down the length of Winthrop Street. Joey would have the album with the photographs of Millie. I'd be trundling along my fiberglass reinforced tennis racquet with the patented liquid core. He accuses me of indifference to everything else. And he's almost right. I don't care about the Baccarat crystal. Or his prints. The early Watanabes mean nothing to me. As a matter of fact, he ought to know I don't give a damn about the racquet either. I'm getting too fat to use it. It's true I really don't know exactly what a prostate is. And I do actually hate the car that he insists on getting resurrected every goddamned year. Transplants of pistons, carburetors, motors, vital organs. Only the shell of the original Studebaker is left. People tell him it's a museum piece. He glows. He's been stopped by individuals wanting to buy it. That's true. I heard it. Oh, this was rich. A veritable laugh riot. The man said, "Ten thousand dollars!" very forcefully, expecting enthusiasm. Instead the encounter left Joey totally depressed. Over time he's spent ten times that much getting surgery for that wreck.

So goes the life of sin. To think we gave up all the excitement of our original identities for this good and eternally boring exercise in extra-marital tedium. I call it Janine's revenge.

This afternoon I said, "Joey, let's go out tonight."

He puffed out his cheeks as if I'd socked him in the stomach. "Out?" he gasped.

"I want to go dancing."

"Dancing?" Great, Joey. Repeat everything I say. God, the boredom.

"I love to dance, Joey. <u>You</u> love to dance. You used to love to dance."

The corners of his mouth turned down. The corners of his eyes. His jowls descended. Everything can turn down on the man. He makes the sad mask of ancient theater and, as I'm his counterpart, I guess everything on me should turn UP ready for the most riotous laugh fest in this century. "I *do* love to dance, Honey," he moaned, "But I've already told you about the over-calcification of my old calcaneus wound."

Yeah, he told me. And told me and told me and told me. An old skiing injury. Believe it or not, Joey used to ski.

"*I* still want to have fun!" I announced futilely and I could see all the corners of his fine chiseled face turn down, down still more. Depths of his personal gravity.

The best I could do with the afternoon was to go over to Pam's. Some fun that is. A laugh of centennial dimensions. More of the same dirge in a slightly higher voice. If I didn't tell you you'd still know in a minute that she's Joey's sister. They are so clearly out of the same box. Her mouth was drooping with discontent when I got there.

Remember little old ladies with blue hair? In their youth they got the curse. Then, in their dotage, they suffered the vapors. One suffering after another. Pam looks like that. She's let her hair go natural. Not exactly blue. She saw an ad for this silver rinse in a magazine. The model must have been about 32 years old. So now Pam has silver hair and thinks she looks just like the model. She invites people to guess her age. It's something like Joey asking strangers how much they would give for his car. They guess right and Pam sulks. She never learns.

She was Janine's friend too. That was a thorn for a long time. She kept that creepy self-portrait of Janine's in her living room for years. Under the naples yellow of the straw hat the paint had darkened and darkened, probably from Pam's stinking cigarettes, but the clear eyes still looked out from under the shadow. Reproach. Joey would never go over there. Janine cast her sharp look over all of Pam's artifacts and Pam's brother and his —- what? What would I be, his bad girl? His paramour? The home wrecker. But after Janine and Milly died there was no more point to it. Pam mercifully retired the portrait to her storeroom.

I never have been able to get used to the flutey voice that pipes out of Pam's big face. Complaints issue forth. The office. A little tart trying to undermine her authority. The parking lot. An old fart that keeps usurping her place and then having the temerity to argue about it. Her rental properties. The gal is loaded so her tenants deliberately sabotage the toilets. For the fun of it, she's certain. Chains of cigarettes. She gets a foot away from my face and twists her mouth around to make a big show of sending the smoke up past me. She's virulent. Her eyelids nictate in the heat of her anger, as they also do when she is leaving out a little of the truth. Pam's that kind of liar. One who adjusts the truth to suit herself. Then her words trail off. She forgot what she was saying. "Anyhow," she says lamely. Or she sticks a few words in from a previous thought.

At least I can unburden a little back at her. She's knows us all so long. She introduced us, Joey and me, at that dance long ago. He was dancing a fast dance the first time I saw him. Nothing like Flip. The first time I saw Flip he was critiquing something at the coffee shop. Nobody was allowed to interrupt Flip.

When Joey danced he was electric. But crowing on the shadowed side, making loud fun, Janine laughed at him in that nasty way of hers. "Twinkle, twinkle, little star!" she cried. "Clap your hands if you believe in fairies!" It carried special pain because she introduced herself as Joey's wife right up to the time she and the baby were killed in the crash. I guess she was beautiful. Everybody used to say that. I only remember how sharp she was…her teeth, her nails, her nose, and her lips with the words coming out like poisonous little darts. Sharp little bones stuck out all over her. There are still snapshots around and people look at them and say, "Is that Janine Fletcher? God, wasn't she a beauty?" while all I can see is sharps, tearing away at Joey maybe because he was so gentle, so venomless that she had constantly to tell everyone that he wasn't really a man.

She'd have liked Flip, I suppose. There'd be a real man for her, cruel enough to be her counterpart. What wonderful hell they'd have made for each other. In my imagination I often put them together. Too bad they never met. Janine turned religious, righteous, making herself into a kind of embodiment of chastity. The blessed marital victim.

Flip's still alive. One Sunday morning I turned on the television and there he was. It was a serious discussion of the economic repercussions of the budgetary disaster, the future of the Social Security system, the true import of the national debt, the fluctuations of the dollar, and other fiascos that might as well be prostate glands as far as my understanding of them is concerned. Flip was introduced as some kind of financial genius. Professor Philip Brimite. I bet he's forever the one who steers his wife along by her elbow, if he has a wife these days. Oh, yes, Flip did give me the divorce all those years ago. Very civilized. It was Janine who wouldn't let go.

I wonder if anyone calls him Flip anymore. The boy wonder is an old fart now. Like a dull rock on that television show. Taking fucking forever to enunciate every considered opinion. Hewn in the face of a mountain. As if anyone cared.

Do I remember things right? There was all this passion. Like a storm. I couldn't function because I kept wanting to touch him. More than being touched by him I wanted to touch him. Shower upon him the benefice of my body. That went on forever, too. Even when we were tearing apart I'd see my hand reach out like an alien part. It would want to ruffle his hair, stroke the nape of his neck, nestle in the juncture of his legs. And, even though he hated me, he would want me to let me. Would that happen if I met him today? The draw of his flesh. The coolness of it. Firm. Firm like a peach. Even while my reaching hand sought to caress him my spirit would be damned because of something like the breakfast table. Yeah. Flip critiquing. Did all the trouble start there – with the eggs? Try as I might I was inadequate. At first he explained with exaggerated patience. Later he would just push the plate away with a grunt. Failed. Failed. Yes, Professor Brimite, I certainly flunked eggs, didn't I? Flip was very civilized when I found Joey. After all, his ego was only a little bit dented. Now he was free to seek the Perfect Egg Cooker. From what he told me earlier on, the Egg Cooker that preceded me had also proved inadequate.

It was Janine that carried on. Scene after scene. She dared scream about love. About propriety. About religion. She made it so he would never see his baby again. She alienated half his friends. Some never came back. Some did. They'd look at Joey's album of Millie and would spot Janine and fawn over her. "Oh, look at Janine Fletcher. I forgot what a beauty she was." Joey never forgot. She was the love of his life.

But she damned us. Over and over. Perpetual purgatory. She condemned us to these twenty years of extra-marital tedium.

Joey just had a spasm in his upper arm. He gave a little cry. He called me, but too late. "It's true" he insisted. "A little muscle there began to palpitate. I could <u>see</u> it. And now there's a funny feeling, a vacant feeling as if there is something's missing in that exact place."

"This is a new one," I remarked. First time this millenium.

"Well, whatever you think, it happened," he said petulantly. "And for all you know it could be something. Something serious."

Discombobulated

THE WAGES OF SIN

When Tony Radstrom was seventeen years old he had the kind of adventure young men dream of. Working a part-time job delivering bottled waters, he brought around the big ten-gallon demijohns. It was a heavy burden but Tony was a strong fellow. He'd roll the dolly up to the houses, detach the empty bottles, and attach the new ones in the stand. He rarely had contact with the customers. On one occasion, however, the lady of the house came to the door. She summoned him in. Tony, a pleasant young man by any measure, always polite and affable, stood uncertainly by the door, looking circumspectly toward the toes of his shoes. He could not help but notice that the woman was blonde, attractive, elaborately made-up, and quite voluptuous.

"I think I may be due to pay you," she said. Mrs. Lowell her name was. At least Lowell was the name on the door.

"Oh, that's okay, Ma'am," Tony said agreeably. "You can send it in. Or pay next time."

"Come in a minute," she said rather abruptly.

He wondered if she going to offer him a cookie.

"Tell me about yourself," she said.

"Well," he hesitated. He had no idea how to keep up this conversation. At least she could offer a cookie, then he might say thank you and fill his mouth up with crumbs. "My name is Tony. Tony Radstrom," he said. It was all he could think of.

"Do you go to school?"

"Yes, Ma'am. I'm a senior at Wilson."

"Planning college?"

"Already accepted at State," he replied.

"Good grades?"

"Good enough." He didn't like to brag but he'd been Dean's List through every high school grade, was a member of the Honor Society, slated for several awards in both science and art at the coming graduation exercises, and already had a full academic scholarship at State. "Okay grades," he assured her.

"Do any sports?"

"Yeah, I'm on the tennis team. And swimming. I do a lot of that. Plus, you know, a little basketball and soccer but I'm not on those teams. Just do it for fun."

"How tall are you?"

Tony was just a little bit uncomfortable. He did not understand the interrogation. Was she just being friendly? Somehow her intense look did not seem like friendliness to him but more as if she were amassing information. Did she want him for some heavy job? Perhaps she'd noticed that it took some muscle to get that big water jug hooked up. "Exactly six feet," he informed her.

She stared at the wall over his head a minute. "Come here, Tony Radstrom."

Years later Tony remembered every detail of that afternoon

She took his hands and gave him a look so particular he suddenly realized that something better than a cookie might be forthcoming.

Mrs. Lowell put her arms around him and pulled him close. Her wrapper slipped open. She took his hands and guided them over her body. Tony's ears rang. He was on fire. The thought certainly occurred to him that this was very wrong, but he was seventeen years old. He let her guide his hands. Her robe slipped down. She was stark naked. Tony's breathing seemed to stop. He drew long breaths. He could not believe this was happening. Guys often talked of situations like this, but Tony had chalked most of it up to bragging or exaggerating, expressing as reality their wildest fantasies.

The afternoon was short and glorious. Mrs. Lowell more than made up for what Tony lacked in experience. She showed him things he would have never thought possible. He felt restored, exhilarated, and they repeated the passionate encounter.

"Come back tomorrow," she said. "I'm going to need you again."

It was the beginning of the wildest time of Tony's life. He stopped by several afternoons a week. She said little but her behavior granted her complicity.

Even after two months passed, Tony could not believe this was happening to him. He felt powerful. He felt beautiful. Nevertheless he remained Tony Radstrom, the son of an overly righteous-minded father, the pastor of a small reform sect. Tony had had a conventional upbringing. He did suffer some qualms. At times he could almost hear his father's condemning voice reverberating in his brain.

But could the whole adventure be so wrong? How could something that felt so good be evil? And what about Mrs. Lowell? Was it okay for a woman to indulge in such wanton behavior? When, haltingly, he tried to sound out her own opinion she said, "I'm divorced. I can do anything I want." And that was about the most information she ever gave him. Actually, they hardly ever spoke at all. Speaking was awkward. Her name was Marjorie. He saw that on the magazine labels that lay about. But she never even told him her name and he was reluctant to use it.

Tony's erotic idyll continued all summer. One day Mrs. Lowell broke her usual taciturn silence. "You are going to college soon, aren't you?" she said.

"In a month," Tony replied. "But it's only up to State. I can come here on weekends."

She laughed. Strange. The first time he had heard her laugh. "Don't bother on my account," she said. "In fact, you don't need to come back at all, Tony. Not even tomorrow." His face crumbled. By way of explanation, all she offered was, "I'm moving away. I'm going back home to have the baby."

For Tony the shock was radical. But what had he expected? He knew they were not in love. He knew there was no possibility of getting married or of continuing their relationship for long. After a time rational questions arose. Tony was a responsible young man. If he was to be a father, what were his duties? Would she let him know? Where had she gone? She had told him nothing. He was baffled but also enlightened. *That's all she wanted all along,* he thought. *She just wanted a baby.* He laughed. It was funny. He had almost begun to imagine himself as sexually irresistible. *I really was just a poor seduced sap!* Between surprise and the deflation of his ego Tony found he was glad that Mrs. Lowell had gotten something out of the affair. He knew he certainly had.

Time went by. Tony went to college. He studied Art and Earth Science. These interests to earned him a lucrative job in topographical illustration. Tony did well. He rose to supervisory positions. His innovative ideas profited the company.

Time never dulled the memory of his youthful affair. He romanticized it. He felt immense gratitude toward the woman who had so very ably initiated him. Never again experienced did sex prove as abandoned and uncomplicated. The memory of those afternoons made Tony more confident and confidence made him popular with girls. He liked girls as friends and as sweethearts and as potential lovers though no girl of his acquaintance ever proved as generous as Mrs. Lowell.

In time he met Viva Starace. She was pretty and affectionate. She had a lilting laugh. They liked each other at once. Eventually they were married in an elaborate June wedding masterminded by Viva's mother. Tony found that convention suited him. He loved it all. He loved Viva and the wedding and even Viva's mother. It was a happy enough union that, in time, produced four beautiful daughters. Tony doted on them. He was a loving man. He thought his life blessed. He grew a little stouter.

One day in October when Tony was 42 years old he received an amazing letter.

Mr. Radstrom, it said. *My name is Dan Lowell. I am your biological son.*

Be assured I have no intension of making any claims on you, or of interfering in your life in any way, but I have need of information that only you can give me.

I hope you will agree to this. Please contact me.

There followed a Post Office box number and a scrawled, angry-looking signature.

The shock was enormous. Winded by the letter, Tony fell back into a chair. A multitude of emotions attacked him. He found himself folding the letter into a tight square as he looked furtively toward the dining room where his girls were studying.

So she had that kid, he thought. *A son!* He was glad. He was truly glad for Mrs. Lowell. And, as he pondered this, he realized he was also glad for himself. He was a loving man. He loved his daughters. There had been no son. Perhaps this Dan would become part of the family, a son and big brother for all of them to love. But what would Viva think?

Viva! If he were to introduce a new family member Viva would be entitled to explanations. And Norma, his mother! How would Norma react to this revenant, the result of a youthful indiscretion of which she probably would rather not know? His father would surely have brought down upon Tony's head all the vengeance of the righteous heavens, but Norma was less rigid, a softer person.

He studied the letter a while. To the point. Not illiterate though he did notice the unusual spelling of *intention*. Perhaps best to meet the boy and establish some sort of a relationship. He wanted a relationship. He just couldn't believe it. A son! Amazing! A grown son.

And so Tony agreed to meet Dan Lowell in a coffee shop on East End Avenue. He was eager and excited. He had elevated the meeting to some kind of spiritual consummation of the youthful episode that was still so vivid in his mind.

He was early that day and waited staring at the door. A few minutes after the appointed hour he saw enter the most shocking apparition. Magnus Radstrom, his own father! He was astonished. The resemblance to his father was incredible. Tony had both loved the old man and feared him. Now a youthful replica was entering the door, striding toward Tony like a prophet of yore.

"Radstrom?"

Almost speechless Tony thrust out his hand but the boy made a sideward move and sat down, either failing to see or ignoring the proffered hand. "Yes. I'm Tony Radstrom, Dan. I've always wondered what happened to you and your mother."

The boy shot him a strange, hard look. "Oh, really?" he clicked. Staccato. It sounded sarcastic.

It made Tony wonder what the boy knew, or thought he knew. "Tell me something about yourself," he said.

"That's not what I'm here for," Dan replied abruptly.

Tony marveled. Even the voice, the impatient manner, was so reminiscent of the old man. "I have to tell you this," he said. "You bear the most incredible resemblance to my father."

"Do I?" Dan said and with the same hard finality. "Now that's the kind of thing I am here for. Tell me about your father. Is he living?"

"No, he died about 16 years ago."

"What did he die of? I need that, family, health and medical information."

"May I ask why?" Tony noted that Dan had taken some notepaper out of his pocket. He took out a pencil and prepared to write. "Left-handed, too!" Tony exclaimed. "Just like Father."

"Well, maybe that's important. I don't know. I need health information about your family. Ailments. Siblings. Relatives. Ancestors, As much as you can tell me."

"Why?"

"Look, Radstrom, this is not my idea. I am engaged to a girl and she is distressed because I know so little about my ancestry. She has harassed me until I promised to do some research. I'm sure you can give me that much," he declared coldly. "A little information."

Not so simple. Tony wanted to ask a hundred questions of his own but he felt an unyielding hostility and settled himself back to produce family history, birth and death, twins, whatever he could dredge up from the family archives in his memory.

Dan sat and scribbled notes. Angry black pencil slashes covering his notepad. "Is that all?"

"Yes. All. Now can you tell me something? What happened to your mother?

"Nice you ask. About time," Dan growled. "She was the best woman that ever lived. She deserved better than you."

Tony let out a puff of air. He could only think of his seventeen-year-old self, innocently pulled toward the wonderful seduction of a woman's body for the first time. "But I…"

The boy leaned toward him. He had the terrible patriarchal look of Magnus Radstrom, eyes drilling anger, voice condemning like a trumpet for the Judgment Day. "I hate you, Mister," he said, "I've hated you all my life."

And Dan Lowell picked up his papers and strode angrily out of the coffee shop.

Tony Radstrom sat for a long time. He studied the menu card but really couldn't seem to read it. He knew that now he could never look back at the adventure of his youth with the joy and uncomplicated pleasure he had once felt.

After all this time his father had caught him out and defined those memories as Sin.

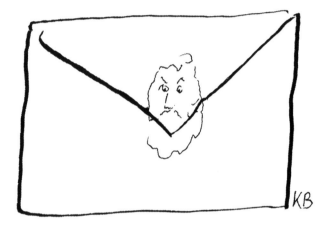

EREBUS—THE WORM

IN DARK OF DARKEST night Gloria Lembo awoke and realized she'd given birth to a long worm. Befuddled by sleep, she understood only that the thing must be hidden from all eyes. Immediately, she stashed it away in a closet. This closet she shared with Suzanne, her sister, who was away at college, so the Worm was not likely to be discovered, at least not before Spring Break.

This incredible event occurred at about three in the morning. Gloria was terribly confused and frightened. Momentarily, she consoled herself with the possibility that she might be suffering from a dream, and she attempted to go back to sleep. No matter how hard she tried, however, Gloria could not pass over the bourn. There was no doubt that something had issued from her loins. Stealthily. Beyond her understanding or her will. Her nether parts could still feel the ghost of that extrusion.

In the penumbra, she stared at that closet door.

Everything seemed so real yet not real. Gloria twisted and raveled herself in the bedclothes. Then she jumped up and examined the sheets. She felt terribly ashamed, disgusted, as if something dirty had been deposited, but the sheets showed no sign of bodily emissions. In loathing, she threw them to the floor and resumed twisting and agonizing on the bare mattress.

In the morning Gloria arose, covered with perspiration. She looked at her hands. They were shaking. Maybe this was insanity. Certainly she understood that the whole concept of birthing a Worm was crazy. Maybe it was a mistake. Perhaps the experience was something in the nature of a very realistic nightmare; a freakish thought that had summoned enough psychic energy to form its own surrogate reality. Sometimes dreams could be strong enough to precipitate actual substance, enough to temporarily distort reason. Dignified men had been known to respond physically to their succubi.

Gloria forced her unsteady legs to go to the closet. She opened the door just wide enough to peek. And there it was. A Worm! An annelid Worm, like a big garden earthworm. It was about ten inches long. Gloria reacted as if shot. She slammed the door. She leaned her back against it. Her heart pounded. Her face felt hot and red. She felt her gorge rise. She was heaving from the peristalsis of a vomiting fit. No sooner had she reached the bathroom than she retched violently all over the floor.

"A mess," she muttered weakly. "I've made such a sickening mess." But it was more than that. There had to be evil in it, too.

As she cleaned the floor she heard footsteps. From the hall outside the bathroom her mother's voice sounded. "Gloria," her mother said. "What's up? You should see the condition of your bed. Looks as if it exploded."

"I'll fix it in a minute," she cried. It pained her to speak. She was stiff with panic. The thought of her sweet mother entering that room, perhaps discovering the unholy thing, the Worm, was unbearable. "It's okay. I did it on purpose. The sheets got all wrinkly. I was starting to remake it. I'll fix it in a minute, Mama."

Her mother chuckled. "Little Miss Perfect. A wrinkle in the sheets! Honestly, Glo, you're like the Princess and the Pea."

And then Gloria forced herself to walk back to the room in which she had deposited her abomination. She walked as if learning to walk, methodically placing one foot before the other very deliberately. She walked like an automaton. She remade the bed and smoothed the sheets slowly. She made a wide detour in front of the closet door, trying to remember the bed as it had been, the room as it had been. Please, oh please. She tried to remember her world as it had been and could no longer be.

And now her mother's voice rose up the stairwell. It was so strange. That familiar voice now seemed so dangerous. Her mother commanded, "Gloria, come on down. Breakfast is ready."

With the voice a smell of frying bacon ascended. She shut her eyes and squeezed them to ward off revulsion. The familiar smell of the bacon seemed to take a voice. It said, "Hurry. The real world is still going on. You have to insert yourself into it, even if you have to pretend. No one must know."

"Am I crazy," Gloria said aloud. She shook her head. "Not!" Yet she knew she might be.

At breakfast, even though she loved her gentle mother, she dreaded the possibility of talk. This mother had been her friend in the world that was. Yesterday. Now Gloria thought her mother suspected something terrible and she could not bear that possibility.

She could barely touch the food. She hated the sight of it. She forced herself to crumble the bacon into bits. She kept her head low until she could jump up and run out, as if late for the school bus.

In the packed bus Gloria stood toward the rear.

"Hey, Gloria! You don't look so good," said a girl who, in the previous world, had been a friend.

"I'm okay," Gloria replied stiffly. "But I think I'm going to throw up." and that threat of imminent regurgitation served to push the other girl farther from her.

School was a terrible. Gloria did not participate, kept her head down, pretended to be immersed in a book or scribbled random words in her binder. "Erebus," she wrote. "Incubus. Erebus."

She got away with public silence. But the school day had to end. How could she face her family? How could she return to her cursed bedroom? How could she look at the execration she had produced?

She sought refuge in the library and hid herself in a remote and rather dark corner. She leaned her head in her hands over a book. After a few moments some modicum of reason intruded. She began to consider the uncanny experience of the Worm.

A Worm.

A Worm was not even a possibility.

Yet Gloria knew it was there. And alive.

She was not stupid. She had earned straight A's in Biology. This thing that had happened to her was not possible. It took two gametes to produce a zygote, from whence new life. What had she done to permit this aberration? Nothing. No carnal sins. Gloria was a virgin. True, some months ago, before she broke up with Sonny Deutsch, she had fooled around with him a little. Well, maybe even a lot. But they never went all the way. Perhaps her knowledge of biology was not as complete as she thought. She wondered if some magic spark that spurted from the male could penetrate clothing, could turn corners, could fly through the air like a flea. Sonny had certainly been a loose cannon. For exactly that reason she'd had to break up with him.

If something had sired the Worm it could only be something infernal, profane.

Yet, as she was guilty of no carnal sins, she wondered about other sins. Were there worse sins? Sins of intent. Sins of thought. Subterfuges. Sins of insidious and unacknowledged hatred.

And what about that thing, the Worm? It was hers. She had produced it. Did she have responsibilities to it? Did it eat? Should she feed it? Maybe, by now, it was mercifully dead.

Everything was more difficult at home, more complicated than at school. Her parents knew her old self better than anyone. They watched her push her food around without eating. They worried.

"What's wrong? What's wrong? What's wrong?" her mother demanded.

"Nothing," was the universal answer to that eternal question. "Nothing."

She could feel the parents on alert. They didn't like the answer. Not one bit. They were watching her carefully.

She studied, or pretended to study, downstairs, though the desk in her room had been her usual study place. Her father wandered through a few times.

"Glory," he said. "Come watch the television with me. They're doing a special on classical dance. You'd like it."

She would not be enticed. She was obdurate and silent, leaning over a book.

The time came to retire. Gloria did something she had not done since childhood. She knelt at the side of the bed praying, or trying to pray. No words would come. She could not pray. She knew then that she was damned.

Gloria lay on her bed wide-awake. When she was sure her parents were tucked away for the night she finally approached the closet. Her heart was beating so hard it almost hurt. She opened the door stealthily.

Erebus. In darkest night, there it was. It was there. And it was still alive. She squatted beside the open closet door. As she neared she became aware that the Worm was emitting a kind of humming sound, like a cat's purr, but nicer. It was barely audible.

The Worm wasn't so ugly after all, she thought. The color was sort of a peachy pink fading off to a light brown. Some of the lower rings were brown as the earth. She could detect no features except a pair of very small peritrichous black eyes that looked at her imploringly. There was no way to determine its sex.

"I'm sorry," she said. "I'm sorry for whatever I did. I'm sorry for both of us." At the sound of her voice the purring hum grew stronger. She knew the Worm was pleased. It seemed to grow a little fatter as she sat there examining it.

So the time passed. During the days when Gloria attended classes, her mind was elsewhere. Teachers noticed that she no longer volunteered in class. She missed assignments. Then, in the dark night, she waited until the house was sleeping before she crept into the closet to look at the Worm. It was clear to her that the Erebus was delighted with her visits. It emitted its purr louder and louder. She liked the sound. It was soothing. As the Worm purred it seemed to grow even a bit longer. The brown rings were more pronounced on its body. It was feeding on her, feeding on her presence, so much did it love her, so much was it attached to her. Of course it had been attached to her, after all. Part of her body, wasn't it? Hers.

The world that had been was constantly intruding on her world now, trying to force things back into the old mold. Her parents were looking for their little daughter, glorious Gloria. Her teachers were prodding at her mind, trying to awaken their trusty Arista scholar, their former Student Council President, but Gloria would not take the responsibility for any of it, nor could she confess her reasons when frequently, she was dragged out on the carpet and begged for explanations.

Now she lived for her nighttime visits to the Worm. The Worm was all she had. She talked to it after the family had gone to bed and thought she was asleep. Visits were the least she could do. She felt so guilty for having brought it forth. She knew that it thrived on her voice and her presence because of the way it grew before her eyes. It was now assuming a sausage shape but still annelid, still marked with the brown rings. It was really rather pretty, she thought. The little eyes sparkled.

Worm's only visible feature was the ciliated eyes. There was no real way to tell but perhaps it was a girl. If it was a parthenogenic creature that would have to be. But Gloria feared that Worm was not exactly a parthenogenic birth. Something evil within herself had sired this.

Gloria lived as best she could with her secret. The pressure was considerable. She felt the stress of her old world's importuning. Now, except for Worm, she was alone.

After endless interviews and examinations, one day she was called to the office of the Dean of Girls, Mrs. Strower. Everyone was there. Her parents were there. Dr. Cochran, the ancient school psychologist, was there. Gloria and Mrs. Strower had once been great friends. She would have chosen Mrs. Strower as her favorite all-time teacher. Now Mrs. Strower leveled at her those great wide eyes of clearest blue that Gloria had once admired. They were the eyes of understanding and kindness. "Gloria," Mrs. Strower said. The voice was so soothing, so understanding that Gloria began to choke. Tears filled her eyes. Beside Mrs. Strower sat Dr. Cochran with his dark, accusing scowl. "We are only concerned with your happiness, Gloria," Mrs Strower said in tones of purest reason. "Are you happy?"

She was not. It was quite some time since she'd been happy and she feared she might never be again. She had a terrible secret and knew that its weight must bear down upon her for all the days of her life. She could not blame the Worm. The Worm was blameless, innocent. The blame must lie with Gloria herself. How could she stand it? She was sobbing now and words exploded from her mouth. "Mrs. Strower, I gave birth to…" she choked out.

Mrs. Strower sat upright in her chair. Her kind eyes widened in surprise. "You what?" she demanded.

Gloria could not bring herself to say the two words that would complete the sentence.

Mrs. Strower became agitated, almost frantic. "Where, Gloria? When? How did this happen? What have you done with the infant?"

How could Gloria, a nice and intelligent girl, possibly sit in front of her favorite teacher, her beloved parents, even doddering old Dr. Cochran, and utter such unholy and disgusting words as "I gave birth to a worm?"

There was a great flap. Psychiatrists were called. The questioning did not cease but rather became more intense. There were long silences. Gloria's mother cried. Even the police were called because Mrs. Strower maintained that in the history of the school there had been two instances where girls had given birth and deposited their offspring in the toilet or in the garbage disposal. Such terrible things happened in the modern world. None of them could possibly imagine, however, how strange Gloria's experience actually had been. Nor could she ever tell them.

No evidence of a baby was ever found.

Gloria was placed in a very nice resort where she could rest, recover, and eventually perhaps, explain. But she never did.

Suzanne, her sister, did not return from school until the very end of the term. In the bottom of her closet she found a shriveled cord. She thought it looked like the lacing from an old hiking boot.

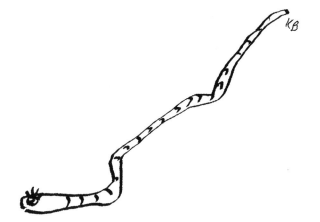

MATERIA MEDICA

BLOOD. A DROP OF blood. A smear. The fears return. Pain, or only discomfort, forcing Henry Tripplet to consider his darkest parts. Who the hell knows what stirrings, what turmoil in the labyrinth of the body this foretells? A twist of the ropey guts? Revolt of very secret slimes in the most vulnerable places?

Sometimes eyes itch. Nasal passages swell. Breath comes short. The hands won't clench. Joints creak. Lower abdomen speaks. What does this presage? Hours can be spent pondering ones guts, assessing twinges, listening to ones intestines. Nothing can be diagnosed but every little anatomical part is cursed with self-awareness, and this is the beginning of hypochondria which is, in itself, a malady.

A bump grew on the end of Henry's middle finger. The nurse called it "the long finger" but some people call it "the nasty finger." He had a little excrescence there before. The dermatologist labeled it a "granuloma," which, to Henry, sounded too much like a breakfast cereal. While he was ready to laugh at it before, it now became more respectable. Anything that insists on growing back must be determined. Determined to undermine him?

Now he thought his health hung on the end of that finger where the node was growing. He wondered — if he let it go, would it bloom into a flower, or a knot, or a knob that could receive intergalactic messages?

The doctor shook his head – always a bad sign. He had excised this thing once before. Didn't look too good for him, so he cast an aspersion on the laboratory. "The lab called it a granuloma," he said, "but I'm not so sure. I think I will deal with it more aggressively."

Aggressively? Not a happy word. Henry saw him take out the long needles. He always deadens the afflicted area but the shot that delivers the deadener hurts more than the treatment. He shot Henry's finger-bud with six shots. The long finger was sick for a week.

What does it tell you about modern medicine? That doctor didn't know. The laboratory didn't know. Do they know this time?

In the days when doctors were still only barbers and sorcerers they might study the roots of your hair, the white moons of your fingernails. Before a thoughtful diagnosis they might smell your breath, your armpits. The contents of your chamber pot would not go unnoticed as they mapped the subtle interconnections of your viscera. Their cures arose from intuition and were miraculous or, sometimes, fatal.

JANUARY MMX

THEY WENT OUT INTO the elements with Key still wearing Angela's greatcoat. Angie, frozen like a shrimp and mad as a jalapeno, kept issuing maledictions or benedictions on everything Key said. It never annoyed him. He knew it was just her way of relating to him. She said, "Damn it, why are we going this way? It's the long way."

"Just enjoy the moon," Key said. "It's a special moon tonight."

Under the Blue Moon an old man sat on the wall and thought his brilliant thoughts. He thought about his death and he smiled at what a pity it was that his head, which was only a small container but infinitely full and everlastingly giving birth to brilliant thoughts, could shut off just like that. All these elucidations, illuminations that ran through his brain, often animated like living things, would cease to exist upon his imminent death. And his death *was* imminent. He knew that because he was a very old man, a logical old man who understood the inevitable decrepitude of bones and flesh and connective tissues.

In spite of the universe of mental activity contained in the little planet of his head he probably looked very stupid, he reflected, because his eyebrows were so thick they overlapped his eyes. An abnormality of his skull caused a ledge of his brow like that of the skull of a Neanderthal. This he knew only from the testimony of women who might have described him out of sheer duplicity. As far as what he actually looked like he never could really tell because he always remained on the inside of his head where the perspective was not only indifferent but entirely oblivious to the matter of appearance.

As Angela spoke Key could see her words as if written on the air. The letters remained connected but quickly dissolved and drifted down through the clear night air with as much direction as truth in running water, as meaningful as the letters in a bowl of soup. Three notes emerged from her as distinct and separate. She was very gutteral, rough in her speech, but musical in song so they had accepted her in the Merryvale Chorus even though she spoke like a croaking frog.

"Keith, for Christ's sake, pay attention!" she demanded, and then she uttered three distinct and very beautiful notes of song, her musical punctuation which arose from a beautiful part of her that Key knew surely existed.

If there were such a thing as the transmigration of souls with any possibility of memory, the old man reflected, then he might a thousand years hence somewhere in the thirty third reincarnation, awaken only to look again into the face of his tormentor who was an old woman, brass voiced much like the young woman now approaching. The old man issued an unintentional cry. He was afflicted with the shouting syndrome. Tourettes.

Angela jumped. Key pressed her arm to offer her the security of his strength and silence. Under the sulphuric yellow of the lights on Hardesty Street her makeup turned to ashes and lead. Wearing the new style of hair made her appear as if they had only half succeeded in her execution. "Watch out for that old geezer," Angela ordered. "He must be up to no good sitting out there on such a cold night."

"Did you know it was a special moon?" Key inquired but he neglected to wait for an answer. "I bet the old man knows."

The old man distrusted the two young people passing him. He was afraid of them. One day young people en masse began to demand their own brand of humor and that was the day vulgarity exploded in the city. Farts reverberated on the innocent air. Little by little more civilized minds became immured to it. The old man emitted a sob for the sad world. He was just an old man that no one paid attention to. He had known women. He had suffered the tyranny of love. Evicted from his home. Now he was free to indulge his thoughts. "You go listen to your damn Shakespeare tapes," she had said to him. "I'll go to bars and listen to the fucking people say fuck. That's the difference between you and me." Instead he went out to listen to the fucking world and she stayed home to drink coffee in the warm kitchen. That was his woman who brewed fake coffee. She stirred in fake sugar, fake cream. A fake woman, the old man thought. He ducked his head away from the couple now nearing.

Angela remained unconvinced. "You're full of shit, Key. The old man probably knows nothing. There's something wrong with him," she muttered. "Why else would he sit out on a cold night? He's as fucked up as we are for taking the long road in the freeze."

"Under the moon," said Key. "You know, it's a special moon."

"They want me sending flyers with the newsletter," Angela complained. "Bertie's in there licking envelopes with her big sloppy tongue, laden with flu or other noxious contagions. Bertie insisted that if I wanted to be part of the group, I must do what the idiot group does. And that's that. How come she always gets her way? Why does everybody do whatever the hell Bertie wants?"

"When there are two full moons in the same month the last one is called a blue moon," Key explained. A riff of cold air passed between them. He wiggled out of the coat and handed it back to Angie. She grabbed it. Key was a slight man, much affected by the cold. In a moment of generosity, Angie had offered him the coat when he stopped by her house. Now she reneged on the munificence. Though she had first offered in kindness she grabbed away her generosity in the need of the moment. Key shrugged.

"Brrr," Key said, but he was smiling.

"Bertie looks as if she is in pain when she sings. Did you ever notice that?" Angie was wrestling into the greatcoat but since she was already wearing a coat she seemed to Key to be growing fatter than ever. "She squeezes her dumb face up as if she's hurting. Well, she gives *me* a sharp pain in the ass."

All the while the most obscene and anti-social thoughts were developing in the old man's head. He considered that they might grow and grow until by dint of community irresponsibility he would offend the civilized world and, ultimately, be released from the agony of his own thoughts by madness.

Angela and Key were walking on Hardesty Street, the street parallel to the main thoroughfare of the town. It was a quiet street, residential. They had almost reached the stone wall, the exact point where the old man was squatting when, like a spasm in the wind, they crossed to the other side.

Perhaps death would rescue him from the madhouse, the old man thought. The lot of them would never realize how important he was. He sat there stolidly, like a pot full of his own unarguable opinions.

"Bertie actually took over the directing last week," Angie complained. "She actually took it upon herself to lead for the encore passage. But I told you about that when I phoned you." Angie said. "We had to look at her idiot face. Thousands of dollars of cosmetic surgery have only made it worse."

"It was the native Americans who first named the moons and they called this kind a blue moon." Key said.

"Don't you remember how she pushed her damn self up in front of the altos? She thinks she's pretty now. She used to have a nose that looked like a saddle."

"There are all sorts of legends and folk lore connected to the blue moon," Key continued.

"You never listen to anything I say," Angela said sharply.

"And we are under a blue moon right now," Key remarked.

Side by side they continued down the long length of Hardesty Street.

62nd STREET

MARIE WEARS A WIG so black it reflects shimmers of iridescent green, as do the feathers of a raven. Her eyes are rimmed with paint, intense as the eyes of Egyptian queens embellished with kohl. From inside this often-smudged mask her actual eyes are a brown so deep they also seem black.

"What color are your eyes, Marie?" I ask her.

"Demitasse," she replies with her characteristic little giggle. That's her charm — her round cookie face, and her little touch of humor. A tinkle of laughter is her trademark. She sparkles as she speaks. Out of a pool of greasy eyeliner her small eyes twinkle like beads of jet.

Marie lives in a one-room apartment near the end of the subway line. The building has seen its days of grandeur. The façade is embellished with wreaths of concrete, garlands of stone. Over the entrance elaborate gothic letters pretentiously proclaim THE SHERWOOD ARMS. Probably in the days of its glory each floor was a spacious apartment but now they have been divided into cubicles like Marie's, each commanding a high rent because of proximity to public transit lines. But Marie has lived here forever so her rent is fixed at an ancient rate. Even so, she can barely afford it.

Marie loves her little domicile. It is chock full of her precious mementos. "My museum," she declares happily, waving her arm. All I can see is a mass of junk and tinsel. She doesn't seem to mind that the building is falling apart. Pipes leak. Mice scuttle in the walls. In my opinion the place should be condemned. It's clearly a fire hazard and there is an impossibly steep flight of stairs to reach the apartment. It is one of those old buildings with fire escapes but if a fire really should start Marie would surely burn to a crisp. The fire escapes demand the agility of a Tarzan and those steep steps are so daunting that, in fact, she rarely emerges from her little den anymore. Her knees are in constant pain. Marie is old.

"You know, Marie, someone should bring your landlord up on charges," I tell her. She laughs. She doesn't agree. She likes her landlord. He stops in the apartment every once in a while and he visits with her, teases her. "Marie, baby," he says, "if I weren't a married man I'd really make a play for you! I told Gus downstairs to be careful who he lets in the building because a lot of these neighborhood bozos have the hots for you!" She reports all this banter to me. She loves it. "You know that Fergesson that tried to come in here once when you were visiting?" she asks. "Last week he showed up right at the door, just as bold as you please, guess what he had the nerve to say? 'Marie, I want your bod!'"

I smile. I bet she loved that. I've seen old Fergesson. He shags along like a bag of unwashed laundry. It surprises me that he can make it up those stairs. He's probably older than Marie and I think she's somewhere in the upper eighties. He's a mess, but he's jovial. He flirts with all women. He's still walking around. That's something.

"Well, Marie, I'm not surprised," I say. You still are a beautiful woman, you know. So? Are you going to take him up on it?"

She makes a disgusted face but she is twinkling. "What? That old fogie? Get outta here! I won't even let him through the door. Yuk! He looks like a toad."

"How old are you, Marie?" I ask her.

"Old enough to know better and young enough not to care," she replies, her voice on the edge of a giggle.

Everyone likes Marie. She has the gift. There is something about her that softens the flintiest people. She is lovable. She wants to laugh. Even Eddie, the landlord, who is a mean old tightwad, succumbs to her charm, but that doesn't mean he'll fix the old radiators and he doesn't care if mice dance the Virginia reel on the worn linoleum floors. The heat works only erratically. The pipes leak. And there is evidence of mouse residence all over the place, even on the little pantry shelves. I know her demitasse eyes really do not see very clearly. She seems oblivious to rodent invasions.

Marie thinks she has a scenic view. Her window looks out on the little yard of St. Ignatius of Loyola Church. It's not much of a scene as the teen-agers hang out there and step on the few plants, and smoke, and litter and tussle and play their raucous music. But Marie sees the green of the grass and remembers her own green days. The view inspires her.

"Last night there were children out there," she tells me. "They walk each other to the subway after confraternity dances. Hand in hand. Boys and girls." She tilts her head up and looks dreamy. She is pensive now. No hint of giggle. "There were two last night," she says, "they leaned against the fence and they started kissing. You know what, Lily? They did it! Right there against the fence! They didn't mean to. They knew they shouldn't. But it was not their fault. They couldn't help it." Marie comes from an era when chastity was the rule, but I think she understands. She looks sad. "They couldn't help it," she repeats forlornly.

I stop to visit often as Marie lives right by my subway stop. She was my mother's best friend and Mama's dying words were, "Lily, don't forget Marie." Sometimes Marie gets confused and thinks I am Mama. Then she calls me Laura. But most of the time Marie is quite lucid and knows exactly who I am.

"Lily, do I look Spanish?"

I look hard at her. In point of honesty, I have to say she looks like hell. That terrible wig is like a cap of patent leather or a carved piece of wood shellacked to a gloss. The pure blackness of it brings out the pallor of her skin and the smudged mascara intensifies the dark shadows of her eyes. She has huge dangling earrings bedizened with dime store jewels of red and gold, her favorite colors, her clothes are of garish, clashing colors. She has a sort of scarf of bright purple with stripes of Kelly green. It's her gypsy taste. Mama always used to scold her for dressing like a gypsy. She'd laugh. "Maybe I am sort of a gypsy, Laura," she'd reply. But with all the terrible embellishments there she is with that cookie face. That round face that always wants to smile. A face I remember through all my years. She's beautiful to me.

"Yes, Marie. You do look Spanish. You look like a hot tamale as a matter of fact."

I am rewarded by a giggle. She likes that description. "Well, I was hot stuff once, honey, would you believe it? They used to say I looked like Dolores Del Rio."

A name out of the past. Who Dolores Del Rio might be is outside my experience but I am familiar with the reported resemblance. I have heard this song before. "Now that you mention it, Marie, I think you do. You actually look a lot like Dolores Del Rio."

She's delighted. "Not now, silly Lily. I meant long ago. When I was young. When we lived on 62nd Street. The boys used to tell me that I looked like Dolores Del Rio. There were so many boys. My brother Paulie's friends. There were always boys at the house. Nice boys. Some of those boys were crazy about me." She giggles.

"Oh, we had such fun on 62nd Street when we were kids. The boys were always around, making us laugh. Laura was always there and we made the boys dance all the new dances. We danced the Big Apple and the Peabody and the Lindy Hop. You should have seen Laura's Lindy Hop. Jack Shannon said she danced as if she was on fire. She was so beautiful. We liked to make the boys dance, and when they wouldn't dance we'd dance with each other. We never got tired. We knew every dance in the book. We knew the Ballyhoo and the Razzamatazz and the Jitterbug. We knew the Bronx Spin and the Coney Island. And we knew the slow dances too, but we liked the fast dances best. We'd get so excited to learn every new one.

"My mother would look in. She always laughed with us. She liked the kids and she liked to see us dance. The boys would kid around with her. Chooky Matha, he was such a cut-up, he made a joke out of everything. He'd flirt with Mother. She always said he was her favorite. Then, when the war came, he went in the Marines and, when he came back, he wasn't funny anymore. We hardly saw him then. He stopped coming to 62nd Street.

"But in the days when Paulie was alive and everyone was young and we lived on 62nd Street there were all those nice boys. They were always sparking me. Joey Kelly said all he wanted out of life was a kiss from me and then he could die happy; so I planted a big smooch on him one day and he fell on the floor and pretended to be dying an agonizing death, like in the movies."

I smile at her old-fashioned use of the word "sparking." "Wasn't there some special boy, Marie?" I ask. Though I know her stories by heart, I think it is my duty to help her tell them. I love her. I can never forget how much she and Mama loved each other. They went through all the dances and the bad marriages and the heartbreak and the sadness together. I can't forget how she sat by the bed during the long and terrible time when Mama was dying. But that was long ago. And 62nd Street was even longer ago.

"Well, there was one boy," she says slowly.

"Who?"

"Varhay."

"Funny name."

"Yes. He was Turkish or Armenian or something. His name was Varhay, but the boys called him Rugger. They said he was a Turkish rug because he was so hairy. If you saw his arms or his body he was covered with hair like a bear. It was more like fur than hair, though. Very soft. Not disgusting. You wanted to pet him. And he was nice. He was very sweet and shy. He had the kindest eyes I have ever seen. The way he looked at me…."

"How?"

"Oh, I don't know," Marie says irritably. "How could I explain? He looked at me with such softness that he made me come to life in a way I never did before. His eyes made me beautiful."

I nod.

"We used to walk out together. Just walk. Hand in hand. Sometimes we'd stop and just sort of lean against each other. I thought my legs would give out. Varhay held me up, stopping where the streetlights made shadows. We'd spoon a little."

"And then what happened, Marie?"

"Then the war came. Varhay's mother put a blue star in the window. After a while it changed to a gold star. That's all."

We're both quiet for a while. Then Marie says, "Those kids last night were so young, Lily. They didn't mean to do anything. They just couldn't help it."

LEARNING TO LOVE CELADON

THE SMELL OF SOMETHING burning. Something both pleasant and cruel in that scent. Like her feelings that had suddenly become so mixed, so confused as she waited for Paul in the coffee shop in the lobby of the Chosun Hotel. Then Ann realized it was the smell, this smell of burning sugar.

Mark had a little habit when they were still in college. He'd slip a sugar cube into his spoon, immerse it in the coffee just enough to let the sugar brown. "Capillary action," he'd say. He always did that. Then he would dump the sugary silt into the ashtray. After a few cups of coffee the ashtray would be awash in granular slime. They had to balance their cigarettes very carefully to avoid drowning them. They smoked. Everyone smoked then. Would his habits have annoyed her in time? He would eventually throw a lit match into the sugar swamp and, momentarily, the residue would ignite. "Cigarette suzette," he used to say. A low, brief, blue flame. That smell would waft up enough to make her cough but it hardly mattered. They themselves were drowning in each other's eyes. Love, love, young love. Mark Gwelt was his name. Almost forgotten. But now, right now, she felt that forgetting was a form of infidelity. He wafted up with the smell, like a wraith of cigarette smoke. So handsome. Curly hair always in disarray. He was square-jawed and shy. He ducked his head while looking at her covertly. His smile was brilliant if a little bit off center. Oh, it all came back now. Reflected in those yellow-green eyes she had become the most beautiful girl in the world, the most valued. It was a first for both of them. They were so tentative with one another. It was a different era. There was no intimacy, only the excitement of the promise of it that was constantly overwhelming them.

A lifetime later she found herself sitting in this place, not a beautiful girl at all but a tired old woman who, just to be presentable, needed her magnifying glasses to put on make-up, even to look just decent enough for her own grandchildren to behold her. Yet with the specter of that smell, Mark's ghost materializing out of it, the beauty she had been at twenty became real again. She felt she could raise her hands to her own cheeks and find them smooth and taut and cool.

Ann smiled. "Smelling memory," she mused. "Proust was right." She hadn't thought of Mark in years. Now the immediacy of his memory made her feel guilty. The great love of her youth. Even in death he had tried to take care of her. He sent Paul. Years ago she and Paul used to talk about Mark all the time. "Remember him forever," both of them thought. An unreal word, forever. A lover's word. He died still believing it. He sent the piece of celadon.

Now she was old and crass and painted like a harlot. In that tranquil lobby she felt ugly and ashamed.

Paul, however, had been remembering. Paul had brought her back to his battlegrounds. It's a wasteland," he warned her. "Nothing grows there." But he was remembering a vanished truth, totally wrong. Korea was beautiful. He said nothing, but he may have been thinking of Mark, who had died in his arms in the fields of a wasteland that was now green and gold with the ripening rice.

They'd driven through emerald countryside, framed by distant misty mountains, towns where ginko trees burst into showers of coins, fields of rice, teepees of sesame, drifts of yellow ochre along the road where grains were dying next to mounds of red pepper. Their guide had said that in this season the polite greeting among the people would be, "Did you make kimchee?"

Paths were lined with cosmos, tall and slender. It was beautiful though Paul would point to gentle fields and say horrible things. "It must have been near here. I blew a man's head off." And Ann wondered if that was all he could see, horrible remnants of blood and old anger, the rage of intelligent young men forced to kill, though she herself saw only the carefully tended crops, or perhaps an old grandfather in a stiff black hat and wispy beard, pensively smoking an incongruous cigarette but still like an ancient scholar of this ancient world.

Ann stared at the hangul letters on the carte d'jour. They had been made feathery with spidery little legs. What did it say in letters that trickled like corpuscles into a capillary? Or like the coffee soaking into the grains of a sugar cube?

Nothing that made any sense to her.

It was Chusok, the time of harvest feast. Through glass that distorted only slightly she saw the rich young Korean girls walking by in their high-waisted hanboks. So beautiful. Like prefect little dolls, holding hands, their dresses in deep purple and ethereal blue billowing so that their very walk was a dance, their progress graceful, joyous. They had never known war. Perhaps they were students even daring, as the students did these days, to disdain the very Americans who had once fought for their freedom.

The only time Mark came home on leave he was wearing one of those officer's hats. There was an emblem on it. It looked like a vulture. She'd stared, hating it. A portent. Foreshadowing, her English teacher would have called it. Shit!

Ann aimlessly stirred her coffee. Where would Paul have gotten to now? Out remembering on his own battles? Choking with that frightening anger over something that no longer existed. Waste. She worried for him. He was not a young man any longer. He could be so rational and then so irascible. She was reminded of their first argument, all because she'd said a word.

"Very nice. Very elegant," he'd said angrily. "I think I've asked you before not to say that word."

"You say it."

"That's different."

"Why?"

"I'm coarse. You're beautiful."

"Shit!"

That was Paul. Holding her forever above all things. He was the product of another age. She loved him very much.

He was a stranger when he had come to comfort her. Of course, she'd already known of Mark's death. She had been notified. She had mourned already. This gruff young man at the door was not welcome.

The reopening of a wound is not. He held in his hands a humble bowl. "From Mark", he said. Mark had wanted her to have it. He held it in two hands like something precious. It was translucent, slick as the jade where the surface held, but cracked all over. "It is precious," he insisted. "Old celadon."

Milky and silky. She hated it. Everything. That it had come from Mark's death effects. Dead. Dead. In anger tears must have started. Just a glaze of tears like the glaze on the crazed celadon. Paul had seen, put out a hand to steady, to comfort her, but instead he started to cry.

Now in the coffee shop of the Chosun hotel she remembered how Paul had stood, those many years ago, a strange young man on her doorstep, crying like a dog barking.

THE TREASURE TEAM

THE TREASURE TEAM WAS in Serrano City last month. Admission was by ticket only and tickets were precious. Dorothy Carty managed to snag two and called me. "Want to go to the Treasure Team with me, Shoney?" Dot knows I'm a huge fan of that show. I watch it faithfully, even repeats. It was worth your life to get those tickets. Believe me, there were people out there ready to trade a kidney for one.

The catch was – you had to bring two treasures.

Dot was even more excited than I, fast losing patience with me the way she usually does. She kept phoning. "Shoney, have you got anything yet?"

I couldn't decide what treasure to bring.

Finally she marched over to supervise a search.

I keep a sparse house mostly because I can't stand clutter. Even so Dot was sure that somewhere in my monastic quarters there had to be an object or an artifact worth investigating. She herself planned to bring an ancient wine bottle and a dresser set. She said it with such a little smirk I knew she thought she had the treasure of the Romanoffs ready to spring on the team.

"So – what the hell is a dresser set, Dot?" I dared to ask.

"It's a thing Victorian ladies kept on their dressers. This one is quite complete and in perfect condition, which counts a lot. There's a mirror, a hair brush, a comb, a button hook, a nail buffer, a little pot holding the powder they used to buff with, a hair receiver, a mirror with a handle, and all of it's silver and sits on a beautiful silver tray worked with repoussé garlands."

"A hair receiver?"

"Yes, a little silver box they kept their hair in. They used to save their hair as they cleaned it off the hair brush."

"Why?"

"You know – they were Victorians, Shoney, very sentimental, very romantic. They'd put samples of their hair in little lockets to give to loved-ones. Sometimes they saved up enough of it to stuff a little pillow for the beloved ones to dream on."

I shuddered. If they were Victorians in those drafty, unsanitary old houses they probably got pneumonia if they washed their hair more than twice a year. I wanted to say, "Yukk," but all I did say was, "Does it still have hair in it?"

"Absolutely! That's what makes the set so valuable. It's intact. The Treasure Team expects no less."

"Human hair?"

"Of course, silly. Sort of a brownish. Probably it was glorious flowing chestnut hair once. Time dulls things."

Yeah. I could imagine. Like a little silver box with a dead mousey thing inside. Maybe the remains of a Victorian cootie in last repose. But I said nothing. You don't want to deflate Dot Carty when she's expanding. She gets regal. Commanding. Full of the triumph and the power of two tickets to the Treasure Team Show.

"Shoney, let's get on with this now," she said impatiently. I hope you're not going to go all poky and indecisive about this thing like you always do. Getting these blooming tickets cost me more headaches than you can imagine.

That's Dot. Drunk on ticket power. She was on a royal toot. She started digging around my house making a mess all over the place. I do hate clutter.

"You're not going to find anything under the sofa cushions, Dorothy," I said.

She sharpened her voice a little. "You know," she said, "I could have given this ticket to Bart McCluff." Bart was her current boyfriend. She thought so anyhow. I really doubt that he would have any more interest in the Treasure Team than he did in Dorothy Carty, which was not much. From what I could observe at the office his major interests were the racing form, beer, and girls at least twenty-five years younger than he was. Dorothy was as romantic and unreal as any Victorian lady but she knew I would never criticize her taste in men after my own multiple disasters. I divorced Terry because he was so saturated in strong spirits I worried about spontaneous combustion whenever he got near the kitchen stove. And Bo Danziger, the other great love of my life, was such a hypochondriac he developed a consumptive cough while we were watching La Traviata.

Dotty was rooting around like a truffle pig. Finally she extracted a pendant from my old jewelry box. "This looks interesting, Shoney. What is it?"

"I doubt if it has any value, Dotty. I picked it up for a few bucks at a garage sale a couple of years ago."

"Oh, Shoney, can't you make up a story? Many years ago you rescued an old lady and she pressed this into your hand while dying. A mysterious recluse left it to you. It was a legacy from a mad countess that…."

"You want me to lie?"

"Do you want to go or what, Shoney? You're not helping the least little bit!"

Oh, I did want to go. I really did. I squeezed my brain. Then a light came on. "I know. Dotty. I have this crazy thing. I hate it but it *is* a crazy artifact."

When I dragged it out of the crawl space above the garage Dorothy curled her lip at me. I knew what she thought. I'd hidden it up there because I couldn't stand the sight of it. Mama had made quite a fuss about giving it to me about twenty years ago when I was in the process of divorcing Terry.

Dot held her breath a minute. She got that penetrating look. Maybe she saw some possibilities to it. "Okay, Shoney, what is the blooming thing? Do you have a story? Tell me its story. The Treasure Team just loves a good story."

"Mmmm. There is a story. But you know Mama. Her stories sometimes come out of her wildest imagination."

"Tell it anyhow. Embellish. Embroider. Make it even fancier. And, while you are spinning the tale, perhaps you can explain the shape of it because you know what it looks like to me."

Oh, I did know.

"Well, I was divorcing Terry…"

"That long ago?"

"Yeah. And I was hanging around Mama's house spreading gloom and hopelessness all over the place. Mama said she had an heirloom present for me. She went in the cellar and dragged up this thing. I was too downtrodden to speak. She told me it was a wonderful thing that had belonged to her greatgrandmother. You know they came over from Sweden sometime in the 1800's? Mama said the pot came with her and I guess they thought it was precious enough to lug over the plains in a prairie schooner."

"Lemme see," Dorothy said. She took it by the handle, very delicately, with the tips of her fingers. "What could it be? A pot? A jug? You know the shape reminds me a little bit of one of those 'shoes' formed in the saguaros when the little owls peck out a hollow for a nest. That's better than the more obvious comparison, don't you think? And look at these little designs around the edge of the opening. Symbols or script of some kind. There's something engraved all the way around. Scandinavian, you say? Do you can think it could be an old runic inscription?"

"For God's sake, Dotty. No way it could be that old."

"Suppose not. What is the metal, do you suppose? Could it be silver?"

"Here. Let me try to shine it up."

"Are you crazy!" she exclaimed. "You know they hate that! They want the original finish on things even if it looks like doodoo."

And that was what I took when one beautiful October day Dotty Carty and I went to the grand gathering of the Treasure Team. The huge old Merton Shanderberg Hall was so crowded there were lines forming even outside the doors. Waiting outside was where the best fun really began. People were standing around with treasures. Soon everyone started milling around to see what everyone else had. You wouldn't believe what stuff was out there. There was every whatnot, trinket, old moldering relic, kickshaw, trifle, vanity, adornment, embellishment, garland, nightstand, commode, festoon, tassel, bijou, gimcrack or antique device. Some people were carrying monstrosities bigger than they were. I was quite overwhelmed by the clutter. "Dotty," I said, "don't look now but I think we're locked into the world's procession of the tchatchkis!"

"Don't get too funny, Shoney," she said. "This is serious."

Everyone around us was craning to see what we had. My peculiar pot drew some strange looks. One goony guy had the nerve to say, "Are you going to demonstrate? Did you bring your husband?" and Dot blinked her eyes as if she didn't understand, but I got it all right, and was more than a little embarrassed. "Damn it, Dotty. Why did I let you talk me into bringing this stupid thing?"

"Shut up, Shoney. Maybe it's a pot for decanting fine wine. Think of it as something like Aladdin's lamp. It's old, that's what's important."

Up wandered a skinny old geezer with a thing that looked like a tapered white rod about five feet long. "What's that," Dorothy asked him.

"It's a unicorn's horn," he announced with perfect seriousness. I could see gawkers gathering to give him a quizzical look. "I know you don't believe me," he said, "but in the XVIth and and XVIIth centuries people had such relics. When I was a boy my father took me to visit his grandfather in France. Grandpere gave this to me. That was way before the war, of course. In his garden the old man had a huge shed full of relics. He had some magical properties in there. Alchemists' retorts. He had the petrified corpse of a basilisk. Oh, how I wish I had that now! God knows what ever happened to his stuff. He died alone there during the war and you know in those country towns the neighbors swoop in like vultures even while you are drawing your last breath. They take everything that's loose. But I think they probably burned that shed because the town was afraid of the occult powers it contained.

"If you look at this horn now – it's definitely something. You can see the striation of hairs all along the shaft. As you probably know horn and hair are the same kind of tissue. Then the horn is absolutely straight, unlike the curved horns common to animals. I've always believed it really is a unicorn's horn, but I see you do not. That's okay. Don't you think it's just as important that, in ages past, people <u>thought</u> it was a unicorn's horn?"

I kept a neutral expression. After all, who's to say how to put material value on past imaginings?

Now more people began swarming up with their precious treasures.

A giant woman appeared. Oh, she was something. Like a proud warship. She had tits like torpedoes. I had to back away. "This has got to be worth a fortune," she boomed. "It is a painting by the very esteemed western painter, Maynard Dixon."

I don't know much about painting but it looked a little over-bright to me. "How old is this painting?" I asked.

"Had to be from some time before the early 40's," she said. "He died in the 40's. But I just got it a few weeks ago. I spotted it in a junk sale in Los Cabritos. There were some Mexicans, probably illegals, selling junk they had picked up all over the place. They had no idea what they had. I snapped up a real Maynard Dixon for only eighteen dollars!" she crowed.

Next one to come wobbling up to see our stuff was a really ancient woman. She could barely totter along. I was concerned about her standing out there in the sun though I have to say it was one of those perfect Arizona fall days, dry and sunny and not hot at all. The old lady was holding a small box. "Is that heavy?" I asked her.

"No. Real light. I'd let you hold it but it's very precious," she said.

"Looks like an old-fashioned papier-maché box to me," Dotty said, rather snottily I thought.

"It ain't the box that's valuable, Sister," she said irritably. "It's the contents. This happens to contain Button Gwinnett's peruke!"

"It's what? A box of buttons?"

She got quite snappish. "No," she retorted irritably. "Button Gwinnett's peruke! Button Gwinnett, one of the original signers of the Declaration of Independence, you dunce! Button Gwinnett, representing Georgia!" At that she carefully opened the box and revealed a mass of really repulsive gray matted stuff like long dead spider-webs covered in grungy dust. It made Dotty's hair receiver look positively sanitary.

"Are you from Georgia?" I asked by way of defusing the moment.

"Yeah!" she said, though I could hear the Bronx in her speech thick enough to spread on Ritz crackers.

"This is not only the tchatchki parade," I whispered to Dotty. "It's the procession of greed, deluded fools, liars, and con artists, and here are we right in the middle of it!"

It took about 40 minutes before we reached the entrance. Somehow in the press of people and junk Dotty and I got separated and we didn't get back together until about two hours later when we met outside as prearranged. Dotty came out looking flushed with success. She was busting to tell all. "Oh, Shoney," she said, "that expert told me the wine bottle was an imitation of an antique put out in quantity by a French vintner back in the 60's. No special value. But the dresser set! It wasn't dramatic enough to get me on the televised show, still, the guy told me, it was worth four maybe as much as five hundred dollars!"

"That's great! So are you going to sell it?"

"You bet!"

"Who'll buy it?"

A blank look crossed her face as realization hit.

"Dot, did you see any of the others we talked to?"

"Oh, yeah, Shoney. You'd have loved this. Remember that mammoth female with the guns on deck? The one that bought the masterpiece from the poor Mexicans? She was right near me. When she brought out that painting she said was by the famous western artist the painting guy looked it over very carefully. I think he was embarrassed. Turned out it was a paper reproduction of a painting that someone had pasted onto canvas and painted over with acrylic paints. Worth? Guess. Zero!"

I laughed. "Dot, I was right in line after the nasty old woman with the box of Button Whatsisname's peruke. The rep kept telling her that it was no use if she had no documentation and she kept screaming over and over that it was Button's peruke. What the hell is a peruke, anyhow?"

"I hope they directed her to the city sanitation department. The whole box looked diseased to me." We were both enjoying this. "I wonder what happened to the guy with the unicorn's horn."

"I think he was putting us on, Dot. But if he wasn't they probably trotted him off to the looney bin by now!"

A man coming out must have heard us say the word "unicorn." He stopped short. "Did you see that unicorn thing?" he said. "It was the prize find of the day. It will be on the televised show when it airs in December."

"You mean it actually was a unicorn's horn?"

"I didn't say that. It was an artifact of a kind that con-men of the middle ages carried around <u>claiming</u> was a unicorn's horn. The old guy actually had documents and old photographs from his ancestors' day. They gave it a value of over ten thousand dollars!"

We stood awhile in astonishment, and then Dorothy said, "So. Shoney, what about yours?"

"I was wondering when you'd ask. Okay. The pendant wasn't worth much. He said good costume jewelry might bring twenty five to fifty dollars these days. And the pot... Oh, I thought I'd die. That expert looked really annoyed. He was real hoity-toity with a phony British accent. He said, 'Tell me about it.'

"I said, '*Me* tell you? I was hoping you'd tell me.'

"'Very well, then. It's American. Twentieth century. Base metal with a silver wash.'

"But what is it?

"Then he really got disdainful. He curled his lip. 'What is it? I would venture to say by the shape of it, Madame, that it is a rather fancifully contrived man's urinal.'"

Dotty was laughing like a maniac.

So ends the story of my treasure. There is a little more, though. The next time I visited Mama I faced her with her hokey tale of pioneers carrying the damn thing westward. She got very indignant. "I never told you any such thing, Shoshonna. I was just trying to give you something to get your mind off your everlasting self-pity!"

"Well, what do you say it is?"

"I don't know. My crazy Uncle Otto left it behind when he was visiting in the 70's. I kept it because I thought he might send for it later, but he never did. As to what it is, take a look at it, girl. Wouldn't you say it was probably that crazy old man's pee pot?"

ELEMENTARY LINGUISTICS

WHEN I WAS A kid the f word was not so prevalent though I think I may have seen it once or twice, chalked on a wall or park bench, but I could not have had a ghost of an idea of what it meant until later, in high school, when my concepts ripened and my vocabulary grew to encompass more forbidden knowledge.

Even the s word, a word with a long Anglo-Saxon history, was remote to me in that innocent time. I heard it here and there, infrequently, except for Clifford, my walking-to-school buddy, who used it all the time. The way he used it was equivalent to saying Drat! or Nertz! or Darn it! One day when we were walking home from school Clifford told me a chalk joke. We often carried chalk for sidewalk games or to mess up clean areas of the street.

"Once there was a cat," Clifford said, and he drew a rudimentary cat's head on the pavement, sort of a box with pointed ears and big round staring eyes. "Its name was Tommy." The cat's head perched on a big T. "And there was a snake," Clifford added as a high S shape unfurled itself from his chalk stub. "And the snake wanted to go to the cat's house to eat the cat, so it climbed up a tree." A vertical line went up beside the T for Tommy to the left of the cat's head. "Whoops. It fell," said Clifford, as he let the chalk slide about halfway down the line where he made a short horizontal line to which he affixed another long vertical. "Then he jumped over to Tommy the cat." An expressive dot like the bottom of an exclamation point went on the spot where the snake jumped. But the clumsy creature fell again, slid down a straight line under the dot. Clifford examined it all as he rose from the pavement and looked at me with a certain air of artistic satisfaction. He smiled. "Well, what does

141

it say?" he asked me. I stared. Did it say something? Sure it did! Big as the snake's tracks on the pebbly pavement. there it was —

S – H – I – T

Spelled out in chalk letters — Clifford's favorite word.

I was delighted. It had all the elements. It was a word story. I did love words. It had a beginning, middle, and a surprise conclusion worthy of an O. Henry tale. It had certain narrative flow. There was even humor in the clumsy snake falling all over the place. At the end, it involved some audience participation. And all was illustrated by Clifford's living, if less than artistic, hand.

Great!

At that particular stage of my, life my mental thesaurus contained no meaning for the word "shit." To express that particular thought we kids used "Poo," or "Poop" or, more delicately, "Number Two" or, in the international mode, "Ca-ca." I think some of the bigger boys said "Crap" sometimes, but it was equivocal, more descriptive of boasts and exaggerations.

What a great story! I rushed home. I couldn't wait to tell someone. The first one I encountered was my sister, Loretta. We weren't always friends but I knew I could win her over with such a delightful illustrated story so I grabbed my notebook and a crayon and launched into the marvelous tale of Tommy the cat. Loretta crossed her arms over her chest and listened intently. I guessed she didn't really understand the complexity of the story. Maybe she didn't quite comprehend the word "shit" just as I had not, so I explained, "That's something Clifford's always saying." Loretta uttered not a word, but turned and went upstairs. I scribbled awhile.

A few minutes passed before my mother's voice rang out from above. "Costanza!" she called. Uh oh. Not a very nice tone of voice. She never called me by my Italian name. She hated my name. When she was my loving Mama she always called me Conny.

"What did you tell your sister?" she demanded and the tone of voice wasn't exactly dulcet. But I was relieved, quite thrilled at the opportunity to tell Clifford's story again. I was still holding paper and crayon so I launched right into the interesting tale of the cat and the clumsy snake. Mama was silent. She was looking at me with a particular intensity, a calculating look. When I finished she remained silent. She did not laugh. "Go play," she finally commanded. A few minutes later I heard her imperative summons, "Loretta!" And, from the very tone, knew that it was Loretta's turn for Mama's disapproval, probably justified.

But what had Loretta done in the space of so few minutes? She had been in the kitchen, peacefully gluing pictures into her scrapbook, that's all. All that had happened was that I told her Clifford's wonderful story at which she had been too grumpy to laugh.

WAIT A MINUTE! That story. That word! Loretta had ratted me out over that word! And Mama had figured out that I didn't even know the meaning.

On that autumn day I added a powerful word to my growing vocabulary. But, as that powerful word was added, a little of my innocence departed.

And I kept accruing words.

There was a little girl in my second grade class. Catherine Micelli was her name. She was just a little raggedy kid like all of us. One day she had the bright idea to bring in a poem that was actually by Edgar A. Guest. She probably copied it out of the newspaper. Guest was the newspaper poet. He had an uplifting thought every day.

Maybe she figured she could get some points out of it. Or even just a little praise. The poor kid probably needed a boost. Little did she know that Miss Lipschitz was a daily devourer of Edgar A. Guest's poetry. Miss L. just about hit the ceiling. "Plagiarism!" she screamed. "Plagiarism! Catherine Micelli, you are a PLAGIARIST!" The poor little mooch looked scared to death. Surely she knew she had copied, but she had no idea that she'd committed so serious a crime with such a resounding word to name it. It was probably not only a crime but also a sin and she would have to confess it to Father Donlon on Saturday.

But I, for reasons unknown, had the word sickness. I was excited by weighty and incomprehensible words. So I started to giggle. I giggled at the word and at poor little Catherine Micelli who seemed about to blubber out all her juices, and I giggled over the hot new word.

Lipschitz looked about to hit a new decibel. "Audacious," she declared, looking straight at me. She had enough trouble with me to give cause for this new adjective, whatever it meant. Nothing good, probably. I could guess that from the context. Puffing out her cheeks, Miss L. sputtered, "The audacity! The absolute and unabashed AUDACITY!"

There she stood, red in the face, eyes popping in fury, Micelli right in front of her ready to inundate the class in tides of grimy tears, and, you know, it had to be funny though I was scared to death. Teachers had a lot of power in those days. It wasn't wise to rile them, but it was just too funny. I had to giggle more and more, as giggles breed more giggles, holding on to my desk to keep from sprawling on the floor, desperately needing the bathroom as little girls with serious cases of giggles are wont to do.

There was such a cache of new words brightening that dreary afternoon.

I collected words. Sometimes they provided keys to the strange and mysterious worlds that the adults lived in, worlds so taboo that we could not help but try to enter.

I maintained a well-worn dictionary.

Sometimes words led me on strange paths. Mama's cousins, for example, were all young ladies then. They doted on me which is why they permitted me to hang around in a corner of the room when they entertained their friend, Tootie Caruso. I made myself inconspicuous and got very quiet. Tootie was a big gossip and always worth listening to. Now she was telling about Larry LoBosco. They all knew Larry and they all thought he was related to the god Apollo. But there was something amiss. I could tell by the lowered voices, the nervous glances in my direction, the closeness of their murmuring heads. "He's been seeing Camille." Tootie said.

"Mmmm." Grunts of comprehension. Maybe of jealousy.

"And…" said Tootie with a pause that always signified an explosive turn to the conversation, "And he impregnated her!"

WOW! Whatever the heck that was, they all fell back, all the cousins, some with mouths agape. This had to be a big one. I couldn't wait to get home to my trusty dictionary. But unfortunately, my dictionary did not always provide a clear answer. *Impregnable* was as close as I could get. So, then and for a long time, all I could figure out in those innocent days was that Larry LoBosco had walled Camille Clementi up in a tower that could not be assailed by either siege or cannon shot.

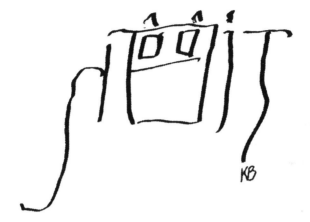

LORETTA

SOMETIMES I THINK OF how fluffed up Mama would get when Loretta wouldn't make her bed. Loretta would just slip out the door, whistling. Oh, Loretta was bold. But she got away with murder, and I followed. "You must never go out until the bed is made, Mama would say. There was a good reason why, too. Supposing you reached the bottom of the stairs, and you fell or you had an attack of something? The neighbors would have to come to carry you upstairs to your room. And what would they see there? An unmade bed!

Che brutta figura!

But Loretta was such a bad girl. She would still insist on sneaking out with the bed totally disheveled, and when Mama came fulminating after her, she'd say, "What kind of attack, Mama? An attack of what? An attack of bees? An attack of hiccups? And she would hiccup about an hour until I was in hysterics and Mama was afraid she'd damage her glottis.

And what about underwear? Every so often Mama would do an underwear inspection. We knew the reason why, too. The reason for keeping your underwear nice and neat and clean was in case you would be in an accident and the medics would have to undress you. Then they would have to see that you had a safety pin holding your slip strap together or, worse yet, a big fat rip in your bloomers.

Loretta didn't worry about it. She was in a hurry. She held anything together with safety pins or bobby pins or paper clips or whatever. Once, when she was babysitting Domenic Busoni, she took one of his enormous diaper pins to repair her slip strap. You could see it at the neckline, but I think she did it just to rile Mama. Mama ran straight to

146

the bureau. So what kind of underwear would you expect to come out of that miserable rats' nest in Loretta's drawer?

This could be very important: there might be a young doctor, handsome and single. He would note such indications of a lazy character. What man would want a lazy character? He'd be wise to stay away from any young woman whose housekeeping would end up being just as slovenly as her unmentionables.

"Good. Better he should stay away if it's housekeeping he's looking for," Loretta would say. "He'd only find out later than sooner."

Loretta was a caution and the exasperation of our sweet mama's soul. After all, Mama didn't ask for much. She just wanted sweet and docile daughters like there are in story books but hardly ever in real life. What she got was this big brat and a little copy cat brat – me.

Still, she wanted only the best for us. She used to ply us with broccoli and it was loaded with plenty of garlic. Everyone knew that would boost the blood and clear the intestines.

"Gimme some more of the veal scaloppini," Loretta would object. "I don't want to eat stinky stuff."

"But broccoli is good for you, my angel."

"I can't be an angel if I go out smelling like an Italian garbage pail."

"Out? Out? What out? Where are you going? Who's going to smell you?"

"The boys at the church Social Hall, Mama. It's the only place you *let* us go."

But we would go other places too. The bad girl and the bad little follower. When we got to that age Mama really worried about it. Boys could get into the story, and boys were dangerous. Especially since Loretta was a clear case of being too smart too soon.

Wasn't meeting boys what it was all about? Even Mama could not ignore the fact that that's what the church Social Hall was for wasn't it? And church Social Hall did not mean a boy had to be an altar boy, either. Some real thugs went there. The back yard Mafia.

"Stay away from the Italian boys," Mama used to say.

"Why?"

"Italian boys beat their wives," Mama explained. Meanwhile, Papa sat nearby, looking innocent and blinking his eyes. Papa was so gentle he wouldn't even beat a drum.

"You don't want us to marry Italians?"

"Well, I tell my *sons*, marry nice Italian girls," she liked to say. "Italian girls are sweet. They go to Mass. They cook. They have lots of babies and they take good care of them. But my *daughters* – I tell them to look for nice Jewish boys. Jewish boys are good to their wives."

"Cousin Tony's an Italian boy, Mama. You gonna tell him to marry a sweet Italian girl so he can beat up on her? Tell him to marry Julie Ricasanni. She's a four-alarm strumpet."

Mama would frown. She didn't know that word but could guess it meant something bad.

"I bet you want us to marry Jewish boys because your girlfriend, Mrs. Jacobskind, got a mink stole from Hymie."

"Well, is there something wrong with that?"

"Italian boys are the sexiest," Loretta liked to say.

"What do you know about such things, Miss?"

We'd be laughing. We loved to drive Mama crazy. "If I should marry a Jewish boy, how come the Social Hall is all you let us go to? You think I'm gonna meet a Jewish boy in St. Anselms?"

"You're too young to meet anyone yet!"

But Loretta did meet boys. Pretty soon she started dating and Mama could do nothing about it except insist, "At least they should pick you up here. Papa and I want to see the boys you are going out with. I want to see if they look me in the eyes."

"Why should they look you in the eyes, Mama? Oh no, Ma, the boys hate that. You make them crazy. You stare at them. After you give them the once over you give them the third degree."

"Since when?" Mama would reply, indignant. "What is 'third degree?' I just talk nice with them. What's the matter? They have something to hide?"

Well, they probably did, but not much. Just the secret thoughts of their secret minds. Everything was on the up and up. I knew that because I knew Loretta. She could keep all those boys in line.

Just to be a bad girl, however, one day she brought home Kenji Matsuura, the Japanese exchange student. Mama's eyes grew round as tea cups. Kenji came in all formally dressed, nectie, suit, looking like the prince of Japan. As a matter of fact he had not been out of Japan very long. His English may have been halting but his manners were impeccable. He was all formal and bowing. Mama loved it. She was speechless. She didn't even pull out the third degree. She totally admired him.

"Kenji is nice," Loretta agreed. "But the bad boys are more fun."

Hot Dog Shanahan bought a broken down jalopy, and he would drive up outside and blast the horn. Mama would jump out of her socks. "Who is that outside with such bad manners? Is that one of *your* boys?"

"You mean Hot Dog? It's Hot Dog Shanahan."

"He should ring the bell when he wants something. Tell him not to blow our ears out when he comes by."

The next time Hot Dog came calling he tooted as loud as ever.

Mama went to the porch and shouted out real loud, "Frankfurter, go away!"

We both laughed till our sides split.

When Mama got old – and she got to be very old – she told everyone about what angels her daughters had been. "My girls never gave me a bit of trouble," she bragged.

At last she had achieved the golden daughters of her desiring.

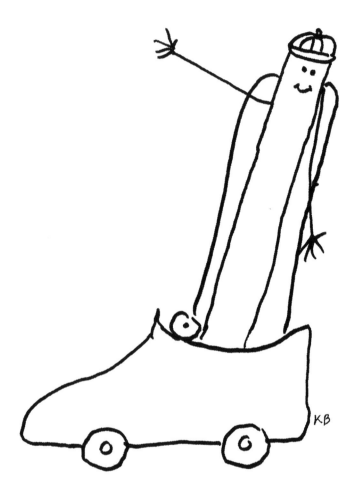

I want to thank Ellie Unruh and the members of the High Desert Writers' group for their invaluable suggestions, and Xo Terra for expert help with the illustrations and the computer..